Sunshine & Cinnamon

LINDSAY ROCHESTER

To request permissions, contact the publisher at AddisonPiercePub@gmail.com

Paperback: 979-8-9881004-0-9

E-book: 979-8-9881004-1-6

Library of Congress Control Number: 2023910152

Published in Ellenboro, NC

Addison Pierce Publishing

LindsayRochester.com

Preface

This book was born during a major time of change for my family. My husband and I decided it was time for him to leave his job and change careers. We spent a large amount of time together as a family, just living life and taking long trips. One such trip took us on the long drive from North Carolina to Maine, stopping and spending time along the way there and back. One stop was in Vermont and I was so taken by the beauty that it had to become part of my novel.

As we traversed Maine, I couldn't take my eyes off the scenery. The novel I brought to occupy my time in the car was left untouched. It was breathtaking, but disappointing in one aspect: We never saw a moose. Do better next time, Maine.

My husband has since started school to become a... wait for it... massage therapist. He made this decision after I had started writing my book, not knowing Chase or his occupation. What are the odds?! I can guarantee you, he will be a most professional and fantastic massage therapist.

For anyone who has gone
through the tough stuff.
I hope things are better now.
If not, keep looking for the sun.

This book's also for my son.
He said I had to use his name,
because I used his sister's name.
However, I never found the right place.
I love you just the same, buddy.
I'll keep my eye out for just the
right spot for you!

1

Chase

Chase Davidson shivered in disgust. His previous client, a woman in her early seventies, was making every effort to set Chase up with her "sexy" granddaughter. He certainly had nothing against said granddaughter; it was her grandmother's methods that made him squirm. Between the innuendo and blatant inappropriate comments, Chase had nearly ended the session early and asked her to leave. He was glad for a break between clients to clear his mind and refocus.

Chase had spent the past six-plus years living in Laurel Falls, a picturesque but largely undiscovered small town in Maine. Most of that time, he was fortunate enough to live in the apartment above The Sweet Spot Bakery, a little shop on Main Street with a vintage feel. The owner of the bakery, Amelia Butler, whom he called Ms. Millie, had become like a third grandmother to him. Her feistiness strongly reminded him of his gran. He helped her out as much as he could and she rewarded him with hugs and far too many sweet treats. They had a good relationship, which had made it extra confusing when she'd given him basically no notice that he had to move out because she needed the space.

Like most people, Chase hated to move. *But at least this way I won't be as likely to develop diabetes.* The thought led him to remember the old commercials with Wilford Brimley. *Dia-bee-tus.* Chase chuckled to himself. He had found a small house for rent on the edge of town at an incredible deal because the wealthy owner had a generous heart.

Since moving from his hometown in North Carolina, he had been working as a massage therapist at the Laurel Falls Spa, a full-service spa in a beautiful white Victorian house. He'd quickly become a favorite among the town's massage-needing clientele. He was also a favorite among the young women of the town, who were excited to have another male to choose from. He, however, never let them choose him. He had tried casual dating when he'd arrived in town, but he'd quickly realized that that wasn't the best idea living in such an isolated small town. Chase avoided all the sidelong glances, stepped back from all the touches, and redirected all the flirtatious conversations. Casual didn't work and he was leery of getting too close in a relationship. The possibility of loss seemed too great. The whole risk versus reward thing often didn't come out in reward's favor.

Chase was often found with world-renowned artist Ryan Kishlar, a man with whom he knew there was no possibility of getting too close. Mr. Kishlar had, in fact, been the greatest draw for his move to Laurel Falls. He was Chase's favorite painter, and as Chase had hoped, Mr. Kishlar had taken him under his wing. That is, if one considers having him clean the art studio and do landscaping as "under his wing." Mr. Kishlar did, however, let Chase observe him painting and offer words of wisdom on occasion, so Chase thought it was probably worth it to get to learn, even a bit, from a modern-day master.

During his break before his last client of the day, Chase sat at a table in the staff kitchen/break room. He sketched an idea he had for his next painting. *It's early morning and the rain from the night before has passed. What's left is dense fog that glows in the early-morning sunrise. Dark, contrasting shadows of tree trunks and rhododendron balance the warmth from the light, and the wet leaves make the colors more vibrant than usual. It's fall, but just barely, so green is still king. The other colors are beginning to make themselves known.*

Chase glanced at the clock, seeing it was two minutes until his last appointment for the day. He stood, stretching his arms and hands, then straightening his shirt. Had Chase known this would be the day his life changed, he would have worn his blue shirt. His mother always told him blue brought out his eyes. He never gave it much thought. Chase walked toward the living room that served as the waiting area for the spa. He spotted his client before she noticed him. He stopped in his tracks, momentarily forgetting how to breathe.

Standing near the sofa, in a stream of light from the window, was a woman whose hair looked as if it contained actual strands of gold. She looked beautifully pensive as she peered out the window. She wore dark high-waisted jean shorts and a top with a subtle floral pattern.

She was the most beautiful woman Chase had ever seen. *I can't believe I got massage oil in my hair during that last massage. What terrible timing. Although it might help to calm it down—it was a little unruly last I checked.* Chase continued to stare, frozen to his spot, his brain putting all of his energy into his eyes. *Her glasses are cuter on her than I thought glasses could be. Her hair looks so soft. And those legs.* He moved his eyes back up her body to her face. *She's a masterpiece.*

When Chase regained some of his faculties, he moved forward and spoke.

"Ruby? I'm ready for you."

The woman looked toward Chase.

"I'm glad you needed a massage today."

Realization dawning, Chase went wide-eyed. He schooled his features as quickly as he could. "I mean, I'm glad you're here. What brings you in for a massage today?"

He smiled his most professional smile and, heart hammering, awaited her response.

"You're *glad* I need a massage today?"

"No, of course not. I wouldn't want you to be in pain or overly stressed."

"That's nice, but then why would you say that?"

"I don't know. I massage a lot of old people and it was a pleasant surprise to see you. I mean, not pleasant, but different. It was different to see someone so beautiful come in. Not that I was thinking about you being beautiful and wanting to massage you. Your body's just different. Tight skin and all. Not that I was thinking about your tight skin. I actually noticed your hair first. I wasn't thinking about how nice it would be to massage you." *Stop talking, you idiot.*

She stared at him, her face a mixture of shock and anger covered by a thin veil of politeness. "I feel like that was exactly what you were thinking."

"It wasn't." *Not exactly.*

She continued to stare at him, seeming to consider her next words or move.

This isn't going to be good.

"This is unbelievable and absolutely unprofessional. You should not be in this line of work if you can't do better than this. Where is the manager?"

Am I about to throw up in front of this woman? How can I fix this?

"I am so sorry. I don't know what came over me. This isn't who I am. The owner isn't here right now, but I'm begging you not to contact her. I really need this job. How about a massage with Janie? On me. She's a very talented massage therapist. She doesn't have any more appointments today, but she owes me a favor. I could make it happen very soon, I'm sure."

"For some reason, I'm feeling a little weird about getting massages right now. I can't believe this—I had heard such great things about this place and *you* in particular. And my back is so tight, so you'll understand if I am more than a little ticked."

"I do. I really do. I can't apologize enough. If you would be comfortable with it, I could work on your back just standing here out in the open. Just until it loosens enough for you to have some relief." *Idiot. Idiot. Idiot.*

Ruby eyed him, considering. She looked toward the window, pushing her glasses up her nose. "You're not going to do anything stupid, are you?" she asked, looking back his way, a stern but rather cute look on her face.

"No. Absolutely not. And there are three ladies cutting hair in the next room, so you could always yell. Although, I promise there will be no need." *Oh my gosh, I've messed up. Please forgive me and let's move on and forget this ever happened. Why does she have to be so cute in her glasses? I wonder if she's a nerd. I'd love that. Stop it, Chase!*

"Yes, okay. I guess I'm desperate, so let's do that. Just know, I will not hesitate to scream," Ruby said with that stern/cute look.

"Noted. Come over here, closer to the hair salon." She moved toward him. "Let me run and grab a ponytail holder to keep your hair out of the way."

Chase took the opportunity during his short journey to the salon to take a few deep steadying breaths and gather himself. *I can do this. I can massage this girl professionally and make her realize that I'm not an awful person who deserves to lose his job. I'm good at what I do and that's why I do it. I'm certainly not a pervert. I can't help it if she's so pretty that my brain stopped working, can I? Stupid brain, get your act together.*

Walking back into the room, he decided it might be a good start to introduce himself. "I'm Chase, by the way. You know, in case you need a name for your voodoo doll."

Ruby scoffed, but he could have sworn he saw the corner of her mouth twitch. She pulled up her hair and he stepped behind her, noting the difference in their heights. *It seems like she's about six or seven inches shorter than me. So that puts her at five seven or eight. Why does that matter, Chase? Focus!* "I'm going to start if you're still okay with it."

"Yes. Go ahead," Ruby said, taking in and releasing a deep breath.

Wow. She really does need a massage and I ruined it for her like a big jerk. I'll give her the best awkward standing massage I can and fix this. Chase took another deep breath. *Mistake. She smells like sunshine and cookies. Okay. Hands on autopilot, brain on something distracting. Tomorrow's to-do list. Buy groceries. Finish unpacking. Well, that certainly sounds like an exciting day off. Maybe Mr. Kishlar will let me come over for a while. Ruby is such a nice name. I should incorporate some ruby into my painting. I'd like to paint her. Look at all the color variations in her hair. I'd have a hard time capturing that, but I'd like to try. I missed her eye color, I'll have to... stop it, Chase! Good grief. Okay, other things. Maybe I should try to plant a garden this...*

"Yes. Right there seems to be the worst of it," Ruby said, startling him out of his thoughts.

"Ah. Yeah, it does feel like it could be the source of your problems. You obviously needed this, I'm so sorry." Chase paused and, when she didn't respond, continued, "What have you been up to that has you messed up?"

"The phrase 'lift with your legs' didn't occur to me until it was too late."

"That will do it. Some heat followed by stretching should help. Maybe some ice before bed tonight. But like I said, I'll get you in with Janie soon. Your contact info is already in the system. She'll give you a call."

Chase continued working in her problem area and he could feel her relaxing under his touch. Suddenly a moan started to slip out of her mouth, but she caught herself and stepped away from Chase.

Ruby had seemed to realize she had relaxed rather too much to maintain her attitude of righteous indignation toward him. She stiffened her posture and pursed her lips. Without thinking, Chase said, "You're going to ruin what we just did."

Ruby looked at him like he was an idiot and left, slamming the door behind her.

Her eyes are like moss just after a good rain.

2

Ruby

Was I too mean? Probably not, he was being a perv. He did seem genuinely nice afterwards, but he was trying to save his job. She decided it didn't matter because she never had to see him again and she was getting a free massage out of the deal.

Ruby was walking from the spa to her grandmother's bakery when her phone rang. She was glad to see the call was from Vera, her closest friend since kindergarten. "Vera, you're never going to guess what just happened."

"Well, hello to you too. Let me think. Did you catch a blue lobster while fishing with a surprisingly well-read lobsterer who also happens to be tall, dark and handsome?"

"Well, that was detailed. And I'm pretty sure they're called lobstermen."

"I'm right, then. When should I come meet him? And are there also lobsterwomen?"

"Vera, there's nobody for you to meet. Mamu made me an appointment for a massage as a thank-you for coming to help. The guy came to call me back and he said he was glad I needed a massage because I'm beautiful and have tight skin."

"No."

"Yes," Ruby sighed, sitting down in a white metal chair in front of the bakery.

"Ruby, that is so disgusting. I think I would have been in shock for a minute before I could have handled it. Did you talk to the manager? Get him fired?"

"No. He was genuinely nice and apologetic afterwards. He said he really needed the job and offered to pay for me to have a massage with the other massage therapist at the spa. A woman. I don't know what's right. It made me wonder if they all think that, and he was the only one dumb enough to accidentally say it." Ruby raised her chin and closed her eyes, enjoying the warmth of the sun on her face.

"I guarantee he isn't the *only* one who would think it. Have you seen yourself?"

"Stop it," Ruby groaned.

"Okay, okay. I'm so sorry that happened to you. If I need to, I can replace his mouthwash with colored toilet water when I come to visit!"

"You're coming to visit! When?"

"You tell me!"

"I doubt it matters, but let me check with Mamu. I'm only here six weeks, so we need to get you here soon."

"Oh, the flexible summer life of a teacher."

"I more than deserve it after the year I had and you know it!"

"Oh, I know. I just hope Mamu doesn't need so much help that you don't have enough time to relax."

"So far it's been really nice being here. Apart from the past twenty minutes, anyway."

"Well, good, apart from the gross masseur, obviously. I have to request time off two weeks in advance, so let me know and we'll make a plan. I gotta run."

"Will do!"

"Love you long time!"

"Love you long time," Ruby replied with a grin.

Her encounter with the massage therapist temporarily forgotten, Ruby headed into the bakery and up to her apartment with thoughts of visiting with Vera. She turned on some music and started what appeared to be some long-overdue cleaning. Whoever her grandmother had living here before her arrival hadn't left the place terribly clean. It was as if he or she had just grabbed their things and left.

She gathered up some trash and carried it downstairs, nearly plowing into her grandmother. "Oh! I'm sorry, I didn't see you with all this stuff in my arms."

"Don't mind me, I'm just your frail, old, pitiful grandmother."

"Oh please. You're about as frail as a grizzly bear."

Mamu grinned mischievously. "Hey, now. I'm still recovering from my surgery."

"Okay, I'll give you that and do my best not to mow you over."

"You're too kind," Mamu chuckled. "I have someone who picks up the trash, so if that's all that is, you can leave it by the bakery trash. He should be coming in the morning."

"Oh, that's nice. Okay, thanks."

"You wanna watch a movie in the RV tonight?"

"Will there be popcorn?"

"Of course."

"Then absolutely I do."

· · • • · • • • · ·

An assortment of movie snacks in hand, Ruby stepped into her grandmother's RV shortly after seven that evening. Expecting to see only her grandmother, she was quite surprised when she was greeted by two smiles. The second belonged to a massive man who seemed to take up half the space in the RV.

He must be a recently retired professional wrestler.

"Ruby, dear, I'm so glad you're here. I want to introduce you to Gerald Jones. He owns Slice It Up, the deli and butcher shop next door."

"Oh. Nice to meet you, Mr. Jones," Ruby said, shaking the man's massive hand.

"He also happens to be my boyfriend."

Ruby, still shaking hands with the man, looked at her grandmother, then back at her grandmother's boyfriend. She tried to wipe the surprise from her features.

"You can call me Gerald. A pleasure to meet you, Ruby. I've heard so much about you." His chocolate-brown eyes seemed to twinkle at Ruby's reaction.

"I'm sorry to say I can't say the same. Obviously," she added, giving Mamu some side-eye.

Whoa. Boyfriend. He looks A LOT younger than her. I wish I could ask. I'll ask her later.

"I'm sorry. I just wanted you to meet him rather than just hear about him." Mamu smiled. She came to his side and he put his arm around her.

"I'm surprised, but happy for you. Wow. So how did you meet? Well, I guess that's obvious since you're work neighbors."

Ruby expected to hear from her grandmother, but Gerald spoke first.

"Amelia came into the shop and ordered a grilled chicken grinder. I told her that we didn't sell grilled chicken grinders, and she asked me what kind of sandwich shop doesn't sell grilled chicken grinders."

"I was merely making a suggestion to help your business. You make me sound terrible." Mamu elbowed Gerald playfully.

Gerald chuckled. "Obviously I didn't think so, because, side note, we now sell grilled chicken grinders," he said, squeezing his girlfriend's shoulders fondly. "Anyway, we got to talking and I learned that she had taken over the bakery. You know your grandmother, she leaves an impression." At this, her grandmother playfully smacked him. "So I showed up at the bakery after a few days. I didn't want to seem too eager."

"Then he came back the next day," Mamu interjected. "He had an idea for a bakery/deli combination deal. Like a special for customers to get a deal for shopping with both of us. Smart idea, huh?!"

"Definitely," replied Ruby.

"We haven't gotten the details hammered out yet," Gerald added, "but we've got our wheels turnin'."

"Hmmm... people could start at the bakery and purchase a meal deal. They get their special bread and a dessert, then go next door where they get their bread filling and a side. Something like that?"

"Yes, exactly! We're just wondering if people will want to do that. Or if I just need to send the bread over and package cookies or some kind of dessert and have special signage." Mamu was smiling as she talked about their idea. She had always seemed happy to Ruby, but this all made her seem next-level happy. *We're never going to get her back to Vermont, are we?*

The trio settled into the tiny space and watched *Star Wars: A New Hope* because somehow Gerald had never seen it. At some point, he said, "How come the guys in the white can never actually hit someone?"

"Nobody knows."

· · • · • · • · · ·

The next morning, Ruby scrambled eggs and ran downstairs to grab a cinnamon roll and some coffee. She stepped out the back door to see if her grandmother wanted to join her for breakfast and ran right smack into a large, solid man and yelped. Ruby stepped back and then saw who it was.

"It's you!" *Freaking gross masseur. I'm proud that I've forgotten his name. What the heck is he doing here?*

"Hi, Ruby. Sorry about that."

"What are you doing here?"

"I'd ask the same, but I think I've put it together," he said, taking in her Star Wars pajamas.

"Yes, this is my grandmother's bakery. I live upstairs."

"Until a couple of weeks ago, I lived upstairs. Ms. Millie asked if I would continue taking out the trash for her. And while she did just kick me out of my home for you, I care for her too much to say no. Those bags get really heavy."

"Oh, so you're the one who left the apartment a mess." *Of course it was him. It's a very gross masseur thing to do.*

"I didn't leave it a mess, but I didn't have time to clean it like I would have liked to," he said, leaning over to grab another trash bag. "She told me not to worry about the mess, that she would take care of it. She felt bad that she didn't give me any advance notice. I assumed she was going to have someone come in and give it a deep clean before the next person showed up, so I didn't do much."

Instead of asking if Mamu needed help or if she could stay there, Ruby had just told Mamu that she was coming to help her because she knew Mamu needed some help while she recovered from her shoulder surgery to repair her rotator cuff.

Ruby sighed, feeling about one percent guilty about the situation. "The stuff that's obviously not bakery trash is mine. Just leave it there and I'll take care of it later today."

"It's really not a problem."

"No, I'll do it. I'm going out there anyway."

"You're going out there anyway? The convenience center isn't near anything. Do you even know where it is?"

Oh, I'll figure it out, you cow.

Ruby stared at him for several seconds, knowing she was defeated, but certainly not accepting it. "Just leave the trash," she said, walking back into the bakery and up to her rooms, not waiting for a response.

When she came down later, her trash was gone. Instead she found a note stuck in a crack between bricks.

I went ahead and took your trash because 'I'm going out there anyway.'
—Chase

I didn't want to remember his name.

3

AGE FIVE

"I'M PRETTY SURE I'M not old enough for kindergarten," Chase said, looking at his mom's reflection in the mirror.

"I'm pretty sure you're just right for kindergarten," replied Chase's mom, Addison, running a comb through his shiny black curls. "Besides, you're going to have the best time! I remember making a piñata in kindergarten. And I know how much you love making things."

He walked into the dining room, where the sun was shining through the big windows, and he felt a bit better. Sunshine always did that for Chase. He sat down in his seat, where one of his parents had already loaded his plate with breakfast casserole and fruit salad. He promptly started picking out the watermelon to eat first.

"Chase, I'm sorry you feel that way, but you have to go in."

Chase looked up in confusion at a woman he didn't know talking to a boy he didn't know. The boy, arms crossed, was staring up at his mother.

Seeing an opportunity, Chase's mom approached and introduced herself and Chase.

"Oh how funny!" exclaimed the mother. "I'm Linda Hershey and this is my son, Chase."

"It's a good name! Is Chase in Ms. Byrum's class?"

"He is. Maybe it would be helpful to these reluctant boys if we all go in together."

Chase was eyeing the other Chase with his stick-straight light blond hair. *He has some dirt on his shirt, I like that.* Chase gave him a tentative smile, which was rewarded by an equally shy smile, and that was that. A friend.

· · • • • · • • · · ·

"Hey, Chase, it's funny that we're both named Chase," Chase said to Chase Hershey while trying to make a roof for the Lego house he had built.

"I was thinkin' you can call me Hershey. Maybe I'll ask the teacher to call me Hershey, too. Might make school better to have candy for a name!" Chase Hershey said, smiling widely.

"I love it, Hershey! Wanna go play with them trucks? There's a park near my house that has a big dirt area and I love to bring my dump truck and excavator and play there. Have you ever been there?"

"Nah, I don't think so. What's an excavator?" Hershey wiped his nose with the back of his hand.

"Come to my house sometime and I'll show you!"

Chase and Hershey sat together on the carpet for story time. They were listening to a story about a pigeon when Hershey whispered, "My mom made chocolate chip cookies and I'll give you one at lunch."

"Hershey, it's not time for talking," said Ms. Byrum.

"I'm sorry, Ms. Byrum."

Chase smiled and nodded at Hershey. Chocolate chip cookies were his favorite cookie. Lost in thoughts about his new friend and chocolate chip cookies, he missed the rest of the story.

At lunch, as promised, Hershey presented Chase with the most delicious chocolate chip cookie he had ever had. The cookie was a bit small, so he ate slowly, not wanting the goodness to end.

"I don't want to ever eat anything else again," Chase said with open-mouthed bites.

"Me neither! Well, maybe still pizza. And ice cream. And candy. What do you think about tacos?" replied Hershey.

"Nah."

"Okay. I won't miss 'em! Wanna be best friends?"

"Yeah, I do! When can you come to my house? I want to show you my Legos. I just made a dinosaur!"

"I'll ask my mom. We have to go to that park too!"

Chase had never had a best friend, but he figured he was going to hang on to this one for a long, long time.

4

Ruby

AGE FIVE

"GOOD MORNING, MY DARLING! It's time to get ready for your first day of school," said Ruby's mom, Nichole, from her perch on the edge of Ruby's bed.

After taking approximately five seconds to acclimate to being awake, Ruby was on her feet. She jumped up and down, already fully dressed, overly excited to be going to school.

"I see you went with a puppy theme for today. An excellent choice, I think."

"I can't wait, Mommy!" Ruby replied. "What do you think they'll teach me? I already know how to read."

"There are always plenty of things to learn. Opportunities to grow and improve. Grab your glasses, your dad is downstairs making pancakes!"

They went downstairs to find three-year-old Charlie already at the table, shoveling in pancakes and eggs.

"Eww! He has syrup on his eggs!"

"This is Vermont. The land of syrup. We should have it on everything," laughed Ruby's dad, Jared, giving her a good-morning squeeze.

.·•·•·•·•·•·.

Filled with the kind of extra confidence that only French-braided pigtails and the perfect outfit can give a five-year-old, Ruby entered her classroom at Green Mountain Elementary. She walked right up to two girls building with magnetic shapes, sat down on the carpet and introduced herself.

They were not interested in being friends with Ruby, nor were the other children she approached afterwards. Deflated, she sat at a table and began drawing a picture of her house, wishing for home, when a girl with French-braided pigtails, jet black to Ruby's golden brown, approached.

"Your hair is really pretty," the girl said with a friendly smile.

"Thanks. My mom braided it. I like yours too. Did your mom braid it?"

"No. My dad did. My mom has tried and tried, but says she doesn't have braiding skills, so my dad learned." The girls both grinned and began coloring together until the teacher called everyone to the carpet.

.·•·•·•·•·•·.

Ruby was beaming when she got to her mom's car that afternoon. Her mother waved as she approached the car. "Hello, darling, I've missed you today. How was kindergarten?"

"It was fun."

"What did you do?"

"I don't remember."

Wow, today was the best. I made one good friend, which is not as many as I thought, but I'll make more later! I think my favorite part was music class. My friend is a good singer! But it was really nice at lunch when she shared her Goldfish with me. Maybe I'll pack something tonight to share with her tomorrow. I wonder if she likes...

Ruby's mother startled her out of her thoughts. "You don't remember anything? How about I ask some questions? Was there anything today that made you smile?"

"I made a friend. She has braids like mine."

"What's her name?"

Oh. Oh! I don't know! I never asked and she never told me. First thing tomorrow, I'm going to introduce myself to my best friend.

· · · ● · ● · · · ·

For dinner that night, Ruby's mom had made Ruby's favorite, homemade pizza with pesto and tons of cheese. They were all sitting down to eat when a familiar voice called from the front door. "Hello, hello! Mamu is here! I came to see how my little namesake liked school today." Ruby's grandmother, full name Amelia Ruby Butler, came bopping through the dining room door. Originally, Mamu was going to be called Granny Millie, but Ruby's one-year-old self had other mispronounced plans. Mamu took on her new identity with great gusto.

"Ruby? Where are you?" Mamu feigned looking around. She was careful not to meet Ruby's eyes.

"Right here, Mamu," she said, laughing.

Mamu looked under the table, up at the ceiling and then finally at Charlie, whom she asked, "Where has your sister run off to?" Charlie threw his head back as he laughed and pointed at Ruby.

"Oh, there you are! Did you just reappear from being invisible? You'll have to teach me that trick! Hello, Nichole, hello, sonny boy," she said, rubbing her knuckles in her son Jared's hair. "I'm sorry I've interrupted dinner. I just got excited about something and came straight over."

"Oh, you're welcome to eat," said Nichole. "There's plenty of salad and pizza in the kitchen. But once you've gotten your food, you have got to tell us about what has you so excited."

"Oh, after dinner," Mamu said, waving in dismissal. "I've got to hear all about school first!"

. . . .

"Okay, so you know my friends from church, Pat and Vivian Collins?" Mamu continued at their nods, "Well, one of their friends is a full-time RVer and they're selling their house and joining him. They got a great deal on an RV and started making their plans with him."

"And how is this exciting to you personally?" Jared asked, concern beginning to show on his face.

"Let's all step outside and I'll show you." Mamu hopped up with a mischievous grin and headed toward the front door.

In the driveway, hitched to Mamu's big black truck, was a silver and white RV. She opened it up to reveal a bed, kitchenette, and was that a bathroom?

This is amazing! I want to live in here!

"So this is Pat and Vivian's RV?" Jared asked with false hope.

"Obviously not, it's hooked to my truck. I've always wanted to see more of the country and now is the perfect chance."

"I don't know, Mom, this is—"

"Perfectly safe," Mamu finished for her son. "I'll be with three other people. And Pat's a mechanic. What could go wrong?"

Wait. What is going on? Is Mamu leaving us?

"You won't live in your house anymore?" Ruby asked, tears beginning to form.

"No, dear," Mamu said, bending to hug Ruby and wipe the tears from her eyes. "But I'll come back often and when I do, maybe I can live in your driveway! Won't that be fun? We've never lived that close."

5

Chase

IT WAS A BREEZY June day, the kind of perfect Maine weather that draws the masses from warmer climates north for a reprieve. Mr. Kishlar had asked Chase to come after work and take a look at the fountain he had on the terrace off the back of his house.

"Mr. Kishlar, I think—"

Mr. Kishlar interrupted in his typical slow way of speaking, "I've told you three hundred times, Chase, just call me Ryan. I don't enjoy the formality of Mr. Kishlar." Ryan, a fifty-something man whose hair was more salt than pepper, had an easel permanently set up outside his home. His property had a breathtaking lake view and some of the most beautiful natural and cultivated land Chase had ever seen. Ryan had set up his paints hours ago and was still working on his latest painting, a magnifying glass view of a painted trillium bloom.

"Ryan, I believe the problem is with the pump. The motor is shot. I could try to fix it, but we would have to order some parts and there's still no guarantee it will work. I think you just need a new motor."

"Eh well, thanks for looking at it. I'll go to the hardware store tomorrow—maybe they can order it for me."

"Yeah, probably so," Chase said, heading over to put the fountain back together.

"Might as well leave that for when you install the new motor."

Sure, I'd be glad to help you out, Ryan.

"Come over here and look at this. Tell me what you think." Ryan beckoned him over, waving his paintbrush.

Chase approached the easel, coming to stand beside Ryan. *That looks just like the ones blooming right there, but larger.* "It looks incredibly real. All the details make it look like a photo. The stamen especially."

"That part actually took me the most time. It was a fine line making them as detailed as necessary without making them the focal point there near the center. Come on, let's have some tea," Ryan said, leading the way toward his house, not waiting to see if Chase would accept his quasi-invitation.

"Coffee?" Chase asked, taking his eyes from the painting and hastening to catch up.

"You know I don't keep that garbage."

Chase smirked as he followed Mr. Kishlar into his house and through to the kitchen. The house was messy as always. He turned on his electric teakettle and before Chase knew it, the house was filled with the whistle of boiling water.

"I got this tea in a tiny tea shop in Tokyo last time I was there. And before you complain, it's loose-leaf, get over it. It's perfectly fine." Mr. Kishlar, despite his fussy demeanor, was clearly enjoying the ritual of tea making.

"Okay. Okay. I'll just pretend it's coffee."

Ryan made a face. "You don't deserve this," he said, handing a beautiful china teacup to Chase.

They sipped in silence for a bit, Ryan closing his eyes when he sipped, fully immersing himself in the experience. *This is actually pretty good. Not that I would ever tell Mr. Kishlar. I'd miss the banter too much.*

"So tell me, Chase, what is inspiring you lately?"

Chase's mind went immediately to the fire-filled green eyes that had shown up in his mind more than once in the past few days. *Why is she sticking with me like this? It's like I've never seen a beautiful woman before.*

"Sunrise," Chase answered truthfully. "Not the vibrant colors, but when the rays just start peeking over the horizon. It seems elusive to attempt to capture, but I'm itching to try."

· · · ● · ● · · · ·

When Chase got home that afternoon, his house felt extra quiet for some reason. Even the dogs were silent, flopped together on the living room rug. He pulled out the ingredients for spaghetti sauce and began browning his ground beef. He chopped an onion, some garlic and the rest of a bell pepper he had been cooking with his morning eggs and threw them in the pan. He seasoned and stirred, waiting on the seasonings to bloom and fill the space with the telltale aroma of a good spaghetti sauce.

Chase opened a large jar of crushed tomatoes and poured it into the pot, leaving it to simmer. He walked to his bedroom, where quite a few boxes were left to unpack. *Okay, today is the day I finish this. I need some tunes, though.*

While living above the bakery the past few years, Chase had gotten used to a certain level of noise. He liked it. Found it comforting, even. While he was generally happy in his new home, he found himself feeling alone quite often. He opened his phone and found his most energizing playlist and got to it.

He hung a few of his favorite paintings around the house and finished unpacking his "miscellaneous items" box before he began feeling hungry and headed back to the kitchen. He gave his sauce a stir and then did a quick taste test. *Perfect.* Then he went to grab the spaghetti from the pantry, only there was no pasta to be found. Instead of being annoyed with himself, he was a bit relieved. Excited to go somewhere, he cut off the stove and grabbed his keys.

· · · · ● · ● · · ·

He was standing in the pasta aisle considering different pasta shapes when something hard lightly brushed his right calf. He turned to see green eyes, which were quickly becoming his favorite, rapidly turn from apology to shock to aggravation.

"Hello, Ruby," Chase said with a grin. "Lose control of your buggy?"

"My *buggy*? You mean my *cart*?" Ruby crossed her arms over her chest. "No, I did it on purpose."

She is so feisty beautiful.

"No, you didn't."

"Obviously not, I don't generally assault people with my *cart* while grocery shopping. Although, had I known it was you, I might have been tempted."

"It's good to see you too, Ruby."

She simply shook her head, arms still crossed.

"Have you ever tried radiatori?" Chase asked, indicating toward a box of interestingly shaped pasta. "I was considering switching it up tonight instead of regular spaghetti."

Ruby looked at him, resigned, then shifted her gaze to the pasta. "I haven't, but it looks pretty good to me. Like all the little layers would hold the sauce nicely."

"I agree," Chase said, snagging a box and turning back toward Ruby.

"No cart?" she asked.

Look at that. She's talking to me.

"Nah. Not getting enough to warrant having a *buggy*."

She gave a half grin and continued down the aisle. He trailed after her, glad to delay returning to his quiet home. "So, what are you shopping for today?"

"Just some basics, since obviously I'm starting from scratch, so to speak," Ruby said. She stopped to grab some diced tomatoes and continued down the aisle. When she turned the corner into the next aisle and he followed her, she stopped. She gave him a look that said, "Why are you following me?"

That's fair. Based on our only two interactions, I'm obviously not her favorite.

"Just grabbing some beans and heading to the checkout." Chase walked over and grabbed an unnecessary can of green beans. "I'll leave you to it, then," he said with a small smile. "See ya 'round, Ruby."

"See ya," she said, and as she pushed her buggy past him, he heard her mutter, "Enjoy your pasta, gross masseur."

6

Ruby

Does he think being super inappropriate to me at the spa and then taking my trash when I asked him not to makes us friends? Wrong, Bozo. Ruby wouldn't really even consider them acquaintances. And what were the odds he just happened to be at the store? She rolled her eyes, bothered by how affected she was by their short run-in. She added a carton of eggs to her cart and headed to the checkout.

Thankfully, he could read her face that it was time for him to move on. *He better not just show up next time I'm in here or I'll think he's a stalker in addition to being a creep.*

"Hello! Did you find everything alright?" The overly cheery cashier yanked her out of her grouchy downward spiral.

"Yes, thank you." Ruby smiled, wondering what her face must have looked like as she approached the checkout. She thought she should try to redeem herself a little. "Have you had a nice day?"

"Pretty good, yeah," the cashier responded as she continued scanning Ruby's groceries. She paused and looked at Ruby with an "I'm telling you a little secret" face, adding, "The best-looking guy in town was just here and I hinted around that I'd like to go to the dance with him."

Oh, good grief. Ruby assumed this was Chase. *He is rather handsome if you can see past his personality.*

She continued, "He either didn't get it or wasn't interested. Although, I think I was pretty obvious. I'm just not brave enough to ask a guy outright. Ugh. Anyway, your total is thirty-six oh nine."

Ruby stuck her card into the card reader. "I'm sorry, I know that's disappointing. Who knows, though, maybe that guy is actually the worst and you dodged a bullet?" *Believe me, it's true.*

"Given his reputation around town, I think he's probably the best, not the worst. I've never heard of him dating anyone, though, so maybe he's just not interested in that at all." The cashier shrugged, handing Ruby her receipt. "You have a great day!"

She glanced down at the cashier's name tag. "You too, Amy."

If this guy had such a good reputation, maybe it hadn't been Chase. However, she hadn't seen another handsome guy around their age there. *Wait a minute, did she say dance? Is this town a giant high school?*

· · · ● · ● · · · ·

Ruby drove back to the bakery and ran into her grandmother as she walked through to the stairs to the apartment. "You have dinner plans, Mamu? I grabbed a frozen pizza for tonight since it's late. You wanna join me?"

"What kind?" Mamu asked with a smile, following Ruby up the stairs.

"I just got a cheese pizza, but I also got a jar of pesto to drizzle on top and I'm going to cut up my leftover chicken from last night and throw that on there."

"That sounds great." Mamu closed the door behind them and followed Ruby into the kitchen space. The apartment was a small space, but perfect for one person living there temporarily. It was entirely open apart from the bathroom. The living space had a sofa and a cozy chair by the window, where she envisioned a lot of reading during her downtime. There was a small dining table between there and the kitchen space. The bedroom area was directly behind the living room, separated by a beautifully painted partition wall behind the sofa.

Ruby turned on the oven and was putting away her groceries when she remembered her conversation with Amy, the cashier.

"I heard there's some kind of dance happening. What's that about?"

"I've been meaning to tell you about that because we're going."

"We are, are we?" Ruby asked, unwrapping the pizza.

"Yes. The last Friday of every month the town chooses a cause to raise money for and then local businesses and individuals donate in various ways to put on this dance. We're making and taking a variety of cookies to sell. Don't worry, though, I can man the table, so you can have time to dance."

"That won't be necessary, I'll be glad to sell cookies while you and Gerald dance."

Mamu rolled her eyes and waved her off. "I'm sure there will be at least one guy who will catch your eye."

"We'll see," Ruby said, pulling a face and getting the chicken out of the fridge. "So what's the cause this month?"

"There's a family who lost their home to a fire about a week before you got here. They have three young kids and they basically lost everything. We hope to fill in the gaps insurance leaves."

"What a horrible situation." Ruby paused, drizzling the pesto. "I'll definitely be glad to help out with the cookies and with whatever else would be helpful. Just let me know."

She was impressed and rather touched that things like this still happened in the world. She was excited to be a part of it this summer. *Maybe I can come help with them some next summer too.*

"Thank you, honey. I was thinking we could get some dough made and scooped into rounds this week. We can stick it in the freezer until we need it next week. We can bake next Thursday and Friday, so they're fresh."

"Sure, yeah. I can make some in the morning. Maybe some browned butter chocolate chip? Those are always a favorite."

"I was thinking about those too. Maybe you could bake just a few for us to taste test. Quality control, ya know?"

"Absolutely!"

· · · ● · ● · · ·

Ruby showered and changed into her favorite oversized sleep shirt. She settled into bed and decided to give Vera a call. She needed to update her on all things gross masseur.

"Ruby Carolyn Butler!" Vera exclaimed happily, answering the phone.

"Vera Ann Stephens!"

"I hope we never greet each other like adults," Vera said with a laugh.

"Maybe this *is* how adults greet each other," Ruby surmised.

"Given the evidence of the last fifteen seconds, I'd say it's likely."

Ruby grinned. She loved the silliness of their friendship. They could be serious and deep, but they always brought it back around to lighthearted fun.

"I talked to Mamu and she said you're welcome anytime."

"Awesome! What if I come for the Fourth and make it a really long weekend? Like the first to the fifth?"

"Sounds great! Hang on, I'm gonna put it in my calendar." Ruby grabbed her phone, which had been lying on the bed near her on speaker. "Oh!" Ruby exclaimed while typing in her calendar. "You'll never guess who I ran into at the grocery store today."

"Hmmm... obviously it was a lumberjack with arms as big as your legs, a twinkle in his eyes and a tendency toward baking when stressed. He was buying cocoa powder because he was out and wanted to make brownies. He was stressed because his shirts no longer fit over his muscular chest and he doesn't want to have to buy new shirts."

Ruby waited a moment before she asked, "Feeling rather loquacious today, are we?"

"I could have continued, but I felt like I was monopolizing the conversation."

"You have an overactive imagination."

"I happen to think my imagination has the perfect amount of activity, thank you very much."

Ruby chuckled, shifting to her side. "I have yet to meet a lumberjack, Vera. Believe it or not, Maine isn't bursting with lumberjacks. But you'll be my first call if I do happen upon one."

"Don't call, send photos."

"I'll see what I can do." *No, I will not.* Ruby knew if she tried to take a sneaky lumberjack photo, she would absolutely get caught. "Anyway, who I actually ran into in real life was Chase, the gross masseur. This is a small place, but what are the chances?"

"You didn't have to talk to him, did you?"

"I accidentally hit him with my cart."

Vera gasped. "No."

"Yes."

"And you're sure it was an accident?"

"Yes, of course I'm sure! I'm not *that* vindictive."

Ruby could tell Vera had taken the phone away from her face because of the laughter she could hear in the distance. When Vera came back to the phone, she was short of breath. "Oh, I sure hope we *bump into him* when I'm there."

"Stop it."

"Tell me what he looks like so I can keep an eye out. Beer belly? Peg leg? Tattooed hair to cover his bald spot?"

"Your creativity is really wasted working in engineering."

"It just gives me excess for our conversations."

"You've certainly put it to good use." Ruby yawned. "I gotta run, I need to get to sleep."

"I wouldn't recommend running if you're trying to sleep."

Ruby sighed, laughing internally at her friend, who had clearly had caffeine too late in the day. "Night, Vera."

"Hang on. What does he actually look like?"

"Black curly hair, blue eyes, tall, strong looking, devil horns," Ruby said, sans emotion.

"If I had horns I would decorate them on holidays," Vera stated as if this were a serious and normal thing.

"Good night, Vera."

"Night, love."

7

Chase

AGE NINE

"Did you study for the spelling test?"

Hershey stared wide-eyed at Chase. "Dang, I forgot. Quick, quiz me."

"Built."

"B-I-L-T."

"B-U-I-L-T. Okay, how about flight?"

"Everyone in your seats," said Mr. Guion. "We're going to do our spelling test first thing and get it out of the way."

Poor Hersh. He forgets everything. Chase wondered if he needed to become his full-time reminder person.

After the test, the teacher had everyone trade papers for grading. Hershey and Chase always traded when the teacher chose to grade this way, but today, Libby, the girl sitting behind Chase, snatched Hersh's paper before Chase was able to take it. The teacher called out the correct answers and asked the children to hand their papers back, then pass them forward to him.

"Kids, stay seated and silent. I'm stepping across the hall to grab something for our next activity. I'll be right back," Mr. Guion said.

As soon as he was gone, Libby stood up and yelled, "Hershey made a thirty on the test!"

Some people gasped, others laughed. A few looked at Libby in disgust. She ignored those particular looks and continued. "What a dummy! He couldn't even spell trouble. What a doofus!"

Chase jumped up. "Hershey is smart," he said, leaning into her face until she sat down. "And he's way nicer than you, you mean-head!" He was nearly screaming by the time he finished. Mr. Guion walked in just in time to hear the end of his admonishment. The class sat in stunned silence.

"Chase Davidson! Come to my desk right now."

Head hung low, Chase slowly walked to the desk at the front of the room.

"Chase, I'm surprised at you and very disappointed. What did I say to the class before I stepped out?"

"You asked us to stay in our seats and be quiet."

"And were you doing either of those things when I returned?"

"No, sir," Chase said, staring at his shoes, embarrassed.

"Can you tell me what happened?" Mr. Guion asked in a voice that was both kind and firm.

"Yes. When you left, Libby stood up and told everyone Hershey's grade on the spelling test. She said all sorts of mean things about him and it made me very mad. So I stood up beside her and told her that Hershey is not stupid and that he's nice."

"I see," Mr. Guion said with a sigh. "It's never a bad idea to stick up for a friend, but I think maybe you could have handled it a little differently. I'd like you to stay for a few minutes after school and we'll talk more about this."

"Yes, sir."

"Thank you, Chase. Libby, please come to my desk."

As Mr. Guion questioned Libby, Chase walked back to his desk, embarrassed red covering his face. Hershey briefly grabbed his arm as he walked past. "Thanks, man. You're the best."

The red left his face as he took his seat, knowing what he had done mattered to his friend.

· · • • · • • • · ·

"Hey, Mom! Can I play video games?" Chase called from his room.

"Have you finished your homework?" his mom answered from somewhere in the house.

"Yeah."

"Have you finished your chores?"

"No." *Ugh, I hate trash/sinks day.*

"Well, there's your answer."

Chase dragged himself to the bathroom and began clearing clutter from the counter. *Mom has too many bottles of stuff. What is firming cream anyway?* And there was one with vitamin C in it—maybe she could just eat more oranges.

"Chase, phone for you," his mom said, sticking her head in the bathroom door, catching him studying her products. She smiled, handing him the cordless.

"Thanks," he said, grabbing the phone and heading to his room. "Hello?"

"You'll never guess what!" Hershey yelled so loudly that Chase had to move the phone away from his ear.

"You're getting a dog?"

"No, and now you made my news feel less exciting."

"Sorry, sorry! What's your news?"

"My science fair project was chosen to go to the North Carolina Science Fair. Mr. Guion just called. He said he didn't wanna wait till Monday to tell me. I'm sorry yours wasn't chosen too."

"Ah, mine never stood a chance. But that's awesome! Do you get to go to Raleigh and present it?"

"Yep. I get to miss a whole day of school."

"Dang. Lucky. If I'd known, I mighta tried harder. I've been too focused on the painting I'm doing."

"Whatcha paintin'?" Hershey asked.

"It's a surprise," Chase answered, smiling. He was painting the two of them from a picture his dad had taken of them playing in the creek near their house. It was the first time he'd tried painting from a photo.

"Alright, alright," Hershey said with a chuckle.

"You still comin' over later? Mom said you could spend the night if you want."

"Yeah, man. What's for dinner?"

"Meatloaf."

"I'll come right after dinner."

"Can't blame ya there. See ya then."

8

Ruby

AGE NINE

"Alright, class, line up by the door," Ms. Whitelaw called from the back of the room.

Ruby got in line behind her best friend, Vera. "Let's go to the swings first," whispered her friend.

"That's what I was thinking!!"

Ruby's recess overlapped with her brother Charlie's, so she got to see him a little every day. Charlie was in second grade. He didn't love school like Ruby did. Nobody could figure out why. He wouldn't talk about it.

As soon as their teacher released them, Ruby and Vera shot off toward the swings. Ruby noticed something going on from the corner of her eye. She glanced over mid-run and recognized her brother's yellow-and-blue striped shirt, then him inside it on the ground. A boy who looked a little bigger than Charlie was bent over him, screaming.

Swings forgotten, she looked around for a teacher, but there were none nearby. She asked Vera to go get their teacher, then ran off toward her brother. As she approached, she heard Charlie crying. "Hey you! Get away from my brother!"

The boy stood up straight and looked at her. "This baby's your brother, four-eyes? Well, your brother got in front of me in line and I'm making sure that never happens again."

Ruby got within an inch of the boy and looked down at him. "He's not a baby. I'm sure he is way better than you are. I'm going to tell your teacher about this. I better never see or hear about you being mean to Charlie again."

The boy turned and tried to run off, but he ran straight into Miss Whitelaw.

Ruby turned and offered her brother a hand to help him up. Trying to control his tears, he threw his arms around her middle. "Thank you. Brandt is the meanest."

Ruby squeezed her brother tighter and said, "You tell somebody if he's ever mean to you again. Okay?"

"Okay," Charlie said, releasing her and wiping at his eyes.

"Has he been mean to you before?"

"Every day," Charlie said, looking down at his feet. "Today's the first time he pushed me down, though."

That boy is lucky that I know I shouldn't hit people. Ruby planned to tell their mom as soon as they got in the car that afternoon.

• • • • • • • • •

It wasn't Mom, however, who picked up Ruby and Charlie from school. When they walked up to the van, which they lovingly called Clifford the Big Red Van, Mamu greeted them with a huge wave and a smile.

"You're back!" Ruby had been counting down the days but wasn't expecting her grandmother for another day at least.

"I couldn't wait to see my two favorite grandchildren," exclaimed their grandmother, turning to grin at them in the back seat.

Ruby couldn't contain her excitement or her questions as she bounced up and down in her seat. "Did you see any bears in Montana? Do they have polar bears? It's cold there, isn't it?"

"Not quite far enough north for polar bears. I did see a grizzly bear mama with two cubs. Thankfully we weren't too close, but I could see them really well with my binoculars!"

Ruby had given Mamu binoculars for Christmas the year before. She loved hearing about her grandmother's adventures and always wanted to give her things to use while on them. One year, she had given her sand toys for her trip to Lake Tahoe. Those had been rather less useful to her grandmother.

"Why are you driving Mom's van?" Charlie asked.

"I'm having some maintenance done on my truck." Mamu turned back to face them as she waited at the light at the exit of the school. "You guys probably won't be interested, but I was thinking we could get ice cream and go to the river."

"We want to!" Ruby and Charlie yelled in unison.

"If you're sure," Mamu said earnestly, smiling at them in the rearview.

· · · **·** · **·** · · ·

Loaded down with waffle cones filled with scoops of moose tracks, everyone's favorite, the three Butlers made their way down the rocky path to the river. The sounds of the river soothed their souls while Mamu was regaling them with stories of her trip to Montana. She had driven well over two thousand miles, seeing all the Great Lakes and more bison than she could count. Her traveling companions had almost hit a bull elk with their RV, which led to an ill-advised jaunt into the woods to see if they could find the elk or his friends.

"Mamu, bulls and elks are two different things," Charlie interjected.

"Bull just means it's male. So it was a male elk," Mamu corrected.

"How did you know it was male? Were you close enough to see his—"

"No," Mamu interrupted. "He had antlers. That's how we knew."

Ruby missed her grandmother terribly when she was gone, but it made her visits all the more special and exciting. And educational, apparently.

The river was the perfect way to spend the afternoon and leave behind the events of the day. Mamu taught them how to skip rocks, although neither of the kids had particular success in that. The three of them jumped from rock to rock across the river, and somehow not one of them managed to get their pants wet.

9

Chase

CHASE HAD ALREADY HAD no fewer than three not-so-subtle ladies trying to get him to take them to the dance next Friday. He had never actually been to one of the town dances, but he always sent a gift certificate for a free massage to be a part of the silent auction.

This month's dance, however, had grabbed his interest, for reasons that he wasn't quite ready to acknowledge. He decided he needed to see Denise Maxwell, the town's unofficial mayor and the event's planner.

"Hi, Mrs. Maxwell. Can I speak with you for a minute?"

"Of course, Chase, come on in," Mrs. Maxwell said, waving him into her home.

Chase took in his surroundings. The home was furnished like he imagined an old-fashioned teahouse would be. There were doilies on the backs of large floral-print chairs, doilies on tabletops and an elaborate floral rug atop pastel pink carpet. *I could get overstimulated in here real quick.*

He took a seat in the light pink rose-covered chair closest to the door, trying to focus on Mrs. Maxwell rather than getting distracted by the quite disorienting wallpaper print.

"Can I get you something to drink?"

"No, thank you. I'm afraid I have to be quick." *Otherwise I might get dizzy.*

"Okay," Mrs. Maxwell said, taking a seat. "What can I help you with, Chase?"

"I was wondering if there's anything I could do to help out at the dance next Friday." *Because I want to be there, but I want to have a reason rather than showing up dateless, seemingly ready to mingle.*

"Oh, lovely! Yes, let's think."

Mrs. Maxwell drummed her fingers on the arm of her chair while staring absently around the room. Chase felt awkward as she was taking an unusually long time to think about his question, leaving him, unfortunately, able to absorb more of the room. There was a china cabinet filled with dolls and gnomes. He'd never seen such a collection. *Chilling.*

"I've got it!" Her sudden exclamation made Chase startle. "You could be part of the silent auction."

"I already sent a gift cert—"

"No, you," she said with a smile. "A date with you."

Chase went wide-eyed. "Oh, Mrs. Maxwell, no. I'm really not interested in that. I was thinking of something that I could do on the actual night. You know, selling something. Standing behind a table. Anything along those lines, really."

"Are you sure, Chase? I think we would get some high bids for you. Think of that poor family."

So now I'm a jerk if I don't do this. Great.

Chase sighed. "Okay, I'll do it. But just this once."

Well, this backfired on me big-time. He wondered if he could take it back and offer a second massage certificate.

"This is absolutely wonderful, Chase! Just wonderful! The team will be so thrilled. The women of the town too," she added with a very strange wink for a woman of her age.

"Glad to help." *Sort of.*

Mrs. Maxwell was oblivious to Chase's lack of enthusiasm. "Just come up with your date idea and let me know. We'll put it on the card with the bidding sheet. We might need more than one sheet." She added that last part mostly to herself as she turned to her thoughts once more.

Chase stood. "I'd better be going, Mrs. Maxwell. I'll let you know about the date plan."

"Thanks so much, honey. You're a good one," she said, patting his shoulder as they headed toward the door.

Chase gave her a kind smile. "Have a good night."

• • • • • • • • • • •

The next day, Chase was in the middle of massaging one of his regular clients, a man named Stephen with chronic shoulder pain, when his thoughts drifted to the date that had been forced upon him. *Okay. What am I going to do that says, "Let's have fun so you don't feel like you've wasted your money, but also I'm not interested in having a relationship"?*

"Ah yeah, that's the spot. Man, that hurts in a good way," Stephen said, groaning.

"Good. Yeah, that should really help if we can get this to loosen up. I'll work on it a little more and then move on and come back to it again."

Too bad Ruby hates me or I'd be hoping for her to bid and win. Although he still didn't want a relationship, so why was he even thinking about it? *What can we do on this fake date?* Given his inexperience with dating, he wasn't sure what a woman might like. *A painting lesson? No, that doesn't seem right.*

"How's the pressure there? I remember this being pretty tender last week," Chase asked.

"It's good. What you did last time really helped it there."

"Nice, I'm glad to hear it."

"Are you going to the fundraiser next week?"

Does this guy have telepathy?

"Yeah, I'm going. I actually have never been to one of the dances."

"Oh, I know. Everyone knows. You've disappointed more girls than you realize. So if you're finally going, you'd better prepare yourself." Stephen laughed.

I may have made a bigger mistake than I realized. Chase gave a nervous laugh.

"Are you going?" Chase asked Stephen.

"Of course. My wife insists every time. She says it's for the cause, but really she just loves to dance."

Chase laughed. He always liked it when Stephen came in for a massage. He had been coming regularly for the past couple years.

"So why have you never been?"

"Well, I'm not a big dancer. Plus I'm not looking for a relationship and I wouldn't want to lead a girl to believe there's a chance, which I feel like dancing could do. I always send a donation, so what's the point in going?"

"You might not believe this, but it's actually possible to dance and not end up married the next day."

"You, sir, are a sage," Chase quipped.

10

Ruby

RUBY WAS SETTLING INTO her life above The Sweet Spot Bakery. She decided she had brought far too much for a six-week stay, but all the little touches from home made the space all the more cozy. *Bringing the basket to hold my most likely unnecessary blankets might have been going too far. It's late June.*

Mamu had not hesitated to throw Ruby right into the bakery as chief baker, cashier and cleanup crew. She was glad for the new experiences as well as the extended visit with her grandmother. She also liked Kelsey, the girl who came in and helped out in the mornings.

Ruby was in the bakery kitchen working on cupcakes for a baby shower happening tomorrow. The woman was expecting her first boy after four girls. *I wonder what his life will be like with four older sisters. Charlie would have hated having four of me.* Ruby smiled, thinking about her brother. He was soon to begin training at the police academy. She worried about him, but it was his lifelong dream to become a police officer, so she had never tried to talk him out of it. Well, not after the first time, when he had passionately told her to mind her business and left.

She was pulling the cupcakes out of the oven when she heard the bell on the door jingle. She walked to the front and had to do a double take because the teen that came through the door looked just like one of her students from her spring Math I class. The girl had caused a seemingly never-ending stream of trouble for Ruby as well as several of her classmates. Ruby could tell her home life wasn't good, but every time she tried to offer any encouragement or help, she was completely rejected.

It was, of course, not her student. The girl smiled blandly and approached the counter. "Hello, how can I help you?" Ruby asked, straightening the display by the register. The girl was looking around at the largely pale pink interior, making a bit of a face.

"My mom ordered some cookies the other day and told me to come get them," the girl said, voice flat.

"Okay, what's the name on the order?"

"Alice Jamison."

"Yep, those are ready. I'll be right back."

When Ruby came back, she found Mamu chatting with the girl, who seemed to be as interested in the conversation as she would be in listening to a history lecture on 1500s personal hygiene. When the girl left, Mamu seemed not to have noticed she had been in a very one-sided conversation.

They headed back to the kitchen, where Ruby started icing the baby shower cupcakes. "Ruby, dear, can you do me a favor this afternoon or evening?"

Ruby paused her cupcake icing. "I might have to move some things around—you know how demanding my social schedule is—but I could probably make it work." Ruby grinned. "What do ya need?"

Mamu smiled at the smear of light blue icing on Ruby's forehead. "I bought a picnic table and it needs to be picked up today. I can't do it because it's bunco night and you know how the ladies get if I miss."

"Yeah, that's no problem. Where is it?"

"Well, it's a bit more than an hour northwest. Will that be okay?"

"Yeah, that's fine," Ruby said, getting a marbled pound cake out of the oven. *Oh, this smells so good.* "I'll listen to my audiobook. Just send me the address. I'm thinking I'll finish icing these cupcakes, then finish up the cinnamon rolls and go. Will that work for me to leave around five thirty?"

"That will be just fine, sweetheart," Mamu said, kissing her cheek. "Thank you so much."

· · • • • · • • • ·

Ruby was looking forward to the drive today. She had tried listening to her audiobook while working, but she was distracted and left out the eggs in a big batch of cupcakes and then she had forgotten the orange juice part of some orange cream icing. The people who had picked up those orange rolls weren't thrilled. Now her policy was music or silence in the kitchen. Unfortunately, that meant she didn't have nearly as much time as she would like for her book.

Ruby iced the last cinnamon roll and was cleaning up when she heard the bell on the door jingle. She wiped her hands on her apron and headed to the counter. Chase was waiting. *Good grief. He can buy his baked goods at the grocery store.*

"Hey. I'm just looking for your grandma. She said she needs a favor—she wants me to pick something up for her."

Mamu!!!

Just then Mamu walked in. "Oh good, you're here."

"Mamu, what's this about? You asked me to go pick up the table," Ruby questioned her grandmother, frustration extremely clear on her face.

Mamu didn't miss a beat. She patted Ruby on the shoulder and said, "I got to thinking that it's probably a two-person job to get a picnic table. Plus, the seller could be a murderer. You never know about these things. And I knew Chase was off this afternoon, so it just made sense."

Oh yeah, this just makes sense. "I'm sure the seller is fine. And I bet they have people who could help me load it," Ruby said, knowing that it was useless.

"I'd really feel better if you went together."

"Don't worry, you can choose the music," Chase offered.

There goes audiobook time.

Ruby sighed. "Fine. Just no country."

"What do you have against country?"

"So much. I take it you're a fan?" *Why did I engage him?*

"I'm sort of an equal opportunity music fan. I figure all genres are going to have songs that are bad and songs that are great. Why discount an entire genre because some of the songs aren't to your taste?"

Ruby looked at him, exasperated. *Why does he bring out the grouchiest part of me?* "No country." She walked to the back, removed her apron and grabbed her purse and water. She never went anywhere without her water.

When Ruby got back to the front of the store, she noticed Chase had Mamu's keys. *Oh, I don't think so.*

"I'd rather drive, if it's all the same to you."

"Not a problem," he said, tossing her the keys.

11

Chase

AGE THIRTEEN

"HAVE I MENTIONED HOW awesome it is being a part of your family? I mean, the vacation perks alone are worth putting up with you." Hershey sighed, relaxing into the hot tub.

"Ha-ha," Chase deadpanned, rolling his eyes and smiling.

Hershey had been joining Davidson family vacations for the past four years. They had been to the Outer Banks, Cumberland Caverns in Tennessee, and Charleston, South Carolina. This year they were in Jekyll Island, Georgia.

"I didn't think spring break was ever going to come so we could get here," Chase said.

"Me neither. You know what I learned in school so far this year?"

"Is there just one answer?" Chase asked with raised eyebrows.

"I learned that I don't understand women."

"Hersh, we don't know any women. We're in middle school."

"Yeah, yeah. But Lina. I'm going to have to have a new strategy when we get back. She seems immune to my jokes."

"Maybe she doesn't like to laugh."

"Everyone likes to laugh."

"Maybe she doesn't like your face."

"Don't be ridiculous," Hershey said with a grin and a wink.

Chase chuckled and climbed out of the hot tub. "I think I'm gonna take my sketchbook down to the beach and see what I can find to draw."

"Is there something we could get to just attach your sketchbook to you permanently?" Hershey laughed. "I'm comin' too. I'll practice for our epic sandcastle. I know you're usually the chief designer, but I have some ideas this year to take it to another level."

"You be the chief and I'll help."

· · · · ● · ● · · ·

Chase and Hershey walked down to the beach, the sun bright and the sky the most beautiful blue. Chase smiled, closing his eyes, facing the sun. He was in the middle of sketching some sea oats near the boardwalk when Hershey ran up with a handful of sand dollars. "You could draw these," Hersh exclaimed, tossing them, somehow artfully, on the sand. "I've never seen so many sand dollars. You want any more, I'm sure I could find some."

"Nah, this is great. Thanks!"

"Someone has to feed your art."

"Feed my art?" Chase laughed.

Hershey shrugged and smiled. "I don't know, man." He laughed, running back to the water.

Chase had never given much thought to sand dollars, but as he drew them, he noticed all kinds of intricate detail. He sketched them from many different angles, noting the different shapes and textures. He was so entranced that he was startled when Hersh plopped down beside him.

"I think I want to be a vet. And I think I would love to work on marine animals."

"That would be cool," Chase said, closing his sketchbook.

"I guess I would have to live near the ocean. Wanna move to the beach with me? We could be roommates!"

"It's a plan! You know how I feel about the beach. Maybe we could become professional sand-castlers on the side?"

"I don't see why not. Dude, remember those sea turtle babies at the Outer Banks? We should look for some tonight."

"Yeah, definitely. I think we should make sure and see sea turtles every year, for our health."

"We should go get ice cream. For our health." Hershey grinned, patting his stomach.

12

Ruby

AGE THIRTEEN

RUBY AND VERA WALKED into Ruby's house after school. They planned to do their homework and get ready for the school's eighth-grade spring fling dance. "I think I'm going to hop in the shower before we start our homework, so my hair has some time to dry. There's some cookies on the counter that Mamu and I made last night. I'll be quick."

A half an hour later when Ruby hadn't shown back up, Vera knocked on the bathroom door. "You alright in there?"

"Ummm... not really?"

"Can I come in? Or should I go get your mom?"

"Yeah, come in," Ruby called. She was sitting on the closed toilet, wrapped in a towel, pressing a huge wad of toilet paper to her leg. "I decided to shave. I haven't done it before and obviously things didn't go well. My ankle won't stop bleeding."

"Nurse Vera here to save the day! I'm thinking a bandage, perhaps medium or large size. Where can I find those?" Vera, who one day hoped to be a nurse, was using her most professional voice.

"Mom keeps them in the kitchen in the cabinet over the microwave."

"On it. I'll be right back."

Vera's the best. I hope this stops bleeding. Ruby was not going to the dance with a giant band-aid on her ankle.

. . . .

Two hours, one bandage replacement and all the homework later, the girls were ready for the dance. The girls got to the school just in time for the Macarena. Vera grabbed Ruby's hand, pulling her to the dance floor. "Come on, I don't want to miss it!"

They danced and had the best time until "Back at One" began to play. That was their cue to get off the dance floor. Vera, who was walking in front of Ruby, made it to the wall. She, however, got intercepted by Adam, a short blond boy who had been in their class last year. *Vera, come save me.*

"Hey, Ruby. Umm… I have something for you." He pulled a box from his pocket and handed it to her. She opened it and inside was a beautiful silver bracelet with red stones. *Surely those aren't actual rubies.*

"Oh wow, Adam. That's beautiful. Thank—"

"Do you want to dance?"

"Actually, I was just heading to the bathroom. I'm sorry."

Ruby speed walked to the wall and grabbed Vera, dragging her to the bathroom. Her heart raced with everything that had just happened.

"What am I going to do?" she asked Vera after stepping inside.

"What do you mean?"

Ruby opened the box to show her friend. "I can't keep this bracelet, can I? I don't like Adam like that. And I think his family is like rich or something, so these could be real rubies. I can't keep something like that if I don't even like him."

Vera was wide-eyed, staring at the bracelet. "You're probably right, but what a cool bracelet. Are you sure you don't like him?"

"Ugh, you know I don't."

"Okay, okay. Yeah, I guess you need to give it back."

"Well, this won't be awkward at all. Come on, help me find him."

The girls stepped into the dark, crowded gym and immediately spotted Adam. Ruby sighed. *Was he waiting for me? Couldn't he have been lost in the crowd so I would have had more time?*

"Adam, hey. I want you to know the bracelet is beautiful and it was so nice of you to get it for me. It's just that I don't really like you like that, so I don't think I should keep it. I'm so sorry." She handed the box to a dejected-looking Adam and gave him a small smile before heading back to Vera, who was, of course, watching from a distance.

"Well, that felt terrible," Ruby said, joining Vera.

"I'm not glad it was you, but I'm sure glad it wasn't me."

The rest of the dance was a blur of fast dancing and moving across the gym to avoid being close to Adam. *At least he's not in any of our classes this year.* They ended up having a great time at the dance but weren't sad to see the end of it. They were getting to have a sleepover in Mamu's RV.

13

Chase

"So do you wanna chitchat or just sit in silence?" Chase asked as he buckled his seat belt. *Am I nervous or something? I could have just let things happen as they happen instead of whatever that was.*

"Did you just say chitchat?" Ruby asked, pulling out, away from the bakery.

Way to start the ride off in the most awkward way.

"My mom says it. I guess it snuck into my vocabulary somewhere along the way."

Ruby huffed out a laugh. "That's fair."

Before Chase could think of anything particularly manly to say to redeem himself, his phone rang.

"Hello?"

"Hi. I have a dog here named Tuck and your phone number is on his tag," a woman said on the other end of the line.

"Oh no. Thank you for calling. Where are you?"

"I've got him now outside Scoops Ice Cream on Clear Creek Road."

"We're not far from there, so we'll be there soon. Thank you so much!"

"Glad to help. See you soon."

Chase ended the call and looked at Ruby. "Would you mind a short detour, and are you allergic to dogs?"

"No and no. I actually really like dogs. What's going on?"

"My dog, Tuck, escaped apparently. He's over at Scoops. You know where that is? It's close."

"Yeah, you'd think I have enough sweets practically living in the bakery, but no. I've already been to Scoops at least four times."

Chase smiled. "Ice cream is its own thing, so that makes sense. Thanks for being flexible. I'm sorry about this."

"No problem. I'd say escaped dogs are pretty high-priority."

Ruby pulled the truck into Scoops' parking lot. Chase saw Tuck sitting in the grass with a woman who looked about his age.

"I'll be right back."

He got out of the car and walked towards Tuck and the woman, who had a good hold on Tuck's collar. "Hi, I'm Chase." He smiled apologetically as he approached. "This escape artist belongs to me."

She smiled, releasing Tuck. "I'm Bridget. Very nice to meet you." She unashamedly looked Chase up and down.

Chase bent down to pet his dog, ignoring her appraisal. "I hope your time spent dog-saving didn't inconvenience you terribly. I appreciate it so much."

"It wasn't a problem at all. In fact, I'm glad it happened," Bridget said with a meaningful smile. He looked up and stood.

"Would you like to get some ice cream?" she added, touching his arm.

"Oh. Thanks, but I'm actually in the middle of an errand for a friend."

"So you're kind as well as handsome," she said, coming closer.

"I try to treat people well," Chase said, taking a step back. "Actually, I'd like to buy you a cone for your trouble, but then I've got to run."

"That's really not necessary, Chase. But thank you, I'd be glad to take you up on that."

Chase held up a finger to Ruby on the way to order the ice cream and asked Bridget what flavor she would like.

"Orange creamsicle, please," she said, sidling up to Chase. *This woman is going to grab me by the arm and try to kidnap me.* He busied his hands getting out his wallet and pulling out some cash.

"What can I get for ya?" asked the Santa-like ice cream man as Chase and Bridget approached.

"One orange creamsicle, one moose tracks and one vanilla, all in waffle cones, please," Chase ordered.

"Coming right up."

When they received their ice cream, Chase bade a disappointed-looking Bridget farewell and headed to the truck, Tuck following at his heels.

He walked up to the driver-side window and Ruby rolled it down.

"Feeling particularly hungry?" she asked.

Chase smirked. "I got vanilla in case you're a purist and also moose tracks if you want to have the best ice cream there is."

"I definitely want the moose tracks," she said, smiling and taking the cone from him.

He walked around the car, helped Tuck into the back seat and slid into the passenger seat.

"And why did you get me an ice cream? Trying to buy my forgiveness?" Ruby asked, petting Tuck.

"Buy your forgiveness? Of course not. What kind of monster do you think I am? One that would eat ice cream in front of a sweet tooth?"

"It would seem not, so good call. We'll have to see about the forgiveness. What's this guy's name? Is he a chocolate Lab?" Ruby backed out of their parking spot and headed toward the exit.

"Turn left here. His name's Tuck. I bought him from someone selling puppies from a box in a grocery store parking lot. I didn't ask many questions because it seemed like they wouldn't have answers. But the vet seems to think he's at least partially a chocolate Lab."

Chase had stopped at a grocery store near Wilmington, Delaware, on his way to Maine from North Carolina. At that time he was feeling lonely, missing Hersh and his family. He was walking out with his single bag of groceries when he noticed a woman getting a box out of her old Corolla with three dark brown puppy heads popping out of the top. He approached the woman and looked in the box. There was one other puppy asleep at the bottom of the box. Something drew Chase to that pup and before he knew it, he had a pet and companion. And a need to go back into the grocery store.

"He's lovely. Reminds me of a candy bar."

Chase laughed. "It would seem that's a high compliment from this one, Tuck. You should be proud." Tuck stuck his nose in Chase's hair.

"Who was your friend, the dog rescuer?"

"She told me her name was Bridget."

"Well, *Bridget* seemed to want to get to know you better." Ruby looked over at Chase with raised eyebrows.

"Eh. I've probably only got space for one woman in my life and Ms. Amelia needs a lot of favors," Chase laughed.

"So it would seem." Ruby shook her head.

"Take a right here. My place is just a couple minutes down this street." Chase pointed. "You can meet my other dog."

14

<h1 style="text-align:center">Ruby</h1>

"LET ME GET THIS straight, you have a chocolate-colored dog named Tuck and a tan-and-white dog named Hershey? I can't be the first person to point out that you made a mistake," Ruby said, giving both dogs scratches behind their ears.

"You're not the first and I'm sure you won't be the last. I had Tuck first. Hershey came about a year later."

Ruby started to respond but got interrupted by licks on the face. She and Chase spoke at the same time. "Ugh, Tuck, stop." "Off, Tuck!"

Tuck stopped, looking pleased with himself. "Bud," Chase chastised, "not everyone is into the face licks."

"Yeah, sorry, Tuck. I'm not a fan," Ruby said, wiping her face with her shirt as best she could.

"Sorry about that. I've learned, as much as I've tried, I'm not a dog trainer."

"Don't worry about it. I can hardly blame him. There was probably residual moose tracks and we both know how hard that is to turn down."

"He could have shown restraint—I mean, I didn't..." Chase stopped midsentence.

"Lick my face?" Ruby raised her eyebrows at Chase. "You were going to say you didn't lick my face, weren't you?"

"Yes, I was," he said, straight-faced. "But I decided that was probably taking it too far."

"Way to show restraint, Chase."

Chase laughed. "I'm going to make sure everything is secure so there'll be no more escaping and then we can head on. Need anything while we're here? Some water? I always need water after ice cream."

"I still have plenty in the car, but thanks. I think I'll use the restroom if that's alright."

"Sure thing," Chase said, pointing. "It's the first door on the right."

Ruby walked to the bathroom. She had been determined to hate Chase only thirty minutes ago. Recent events were making that harder.

Man, his bathroom is clean. He didn't even know someone would be here. Should I peek in his medicine cabinet? No. I wouldn't want someone snooping in mine. Ruby was drying her hands, noting how soft his towels were, when she saw the reflection of a painting in the mirror.

She studied the landscape painting hanging by the door for a minute, then headed back to the living room. *He sure has some beautiful art on the walls.* She came back to find Chase ready to go. She told the pups goodbye and followed Chase back to the truck.

· · · · ●· ● · · ·

"Will you turn on some tunes?" Ruby asked when they were back en route.

"Can do, Captain," Chase grinned.

A minute later, "Lovely Day" by Bill Withers was coming through the speakers. Ruby rolled down the windows and cranked up the sound. "I love this song," she yelled.

"Me too!"

What are the odds he loves this old song too?

They sang and smiled, enjoying the wind in the car. When the song was over, Ruby said, "I just felt like we were in a movie and that song was playing in the background."

"What?"

She rolled up the window and turned down the volume so they could hear each other.

"I just felt like—"

"No, I heard you. I just don't understand feeling like you're in a movie."

"You know, in a movie where there's an upbeat song playing while people are having fun or maybe a more melancholy song playing while someone's staring out a window on a rainy day."

"Were we having fun? Did you just have fun with me?" Chase asked, aiming a silly grin her way.

Did I? I think I did. He was kinda fun and not hard to look at, which helped.

"I had fun with the song and the wind and you happened to be here." *I'll not admit any fun to him yet.*

"Wow. And here I was thinking you were singing the song to me. You wound me," Chase said, grasping his heart.

Ruby glanced his way and rolled her eyes at the dramatics. Chase had really great hair. All windblown, it was especially nice. She'd always liked the black hair, blue eyes combo. *Ewww, stop it, Ruby. He's the worst.*

* * *

With their delay, it was approaching dusk by the time they reached their destination and got the picnic table loaded. They were helped by a man so covered in tattoos, Ruby wondered if he had spent an entire year's salary on his ink.

"How about nineties country for the ride back?" Chase suggested, getting out his phone, grinning mischievously.

Are we music twins? How did he know my one country weak spot? No, I'm not going to give him this. "You know the rules, sir."

"Never mind, there's no service anyway," Chase said, looking at his phone. "We could just see what's on the radio."

"Sure, anything else is fine. Maybe just background noise, though. It's getting dark and I need to focus."

"I don't mind driving if you'd like to swap," Chase said, looking her way.

"No, I'm fine. I'm just always careful."

"Always?"

"In general, yes. I'm thoughtful and generally only take calculated risks."

"I can be that way too, but I also like to be a bit spontaneous. Especially when the outcome doesn't matter."

"Yeah, I mean, I don't sit around calculating everything, but if it matters to me in the least, I think about it."

Chase nodded. "When I was little, my dad and I loved taking drives and flipping coins at intersections to decide which way to turn. We would end up in the most random locations, but it was all about the journey. I loved leaving it up to chance."

I love that. "That's fun. Sounds like you have a good dad."

"I really do."

15

Chase

AGE EIGHTEEN

"GOT ANY GOOD SNACKS?" Hershey asked, rummaging in Chase's pantry after school.

"Nah. Mom's on a health kick. Check the fridge. There's probably yogurt. You could pretend it's ice cream."

Hershey shot him a *yeah right* look over his shoulder. He grabbed some almonds and headed to the fridge. "Guac! And I saw tortilla chips in the pantry. Score!"

"Dad will get you for eating his guac."

"Your dad loves me the most. Trust me, it's fine."

Chase rolled his eyes and laughed.

They were settling in on the couch when Chase's phone rang. It was his mom. "Hey, bud, how was school today?"

"No complaints."

"That's good. I just got off the phone with Gran. She asked if you could come to dinner early, like four thirty. I told her you probably could, but I'd check."

"Yeah, that's fine. Any idea why?"

"She didn't say, but I assume she needs your tallness. Hersh coming to dinner?"

"Nah. His mom is making homemade pizza tonight. You know he never misses that. He's already bragged about it twice."

"I might do it again," Hershey stage-whispered from his end of the couch.

Chase finished his phone call, then asked, "Have you gotten your application in yet?"

"Finished it up last night and submitted it. Man, it was tedious, but it'll be worth it when we're off at school together!" Hersh high-fived Chase. "We've gotta decide if we want to live on campus or off in that apartment complex. I was thinking on campus because maybe we could sleep later. I heard freshmen end up stuck with a bunch of eight o'clock classes."

"I'm not against that. Living on campus," Chase clarified. "I'm definitely against eight o'clock classes."

"We're going to be living the dream," Hersh said, relaxing back on the sofa, a smile on his face.

· · · • · • · · ·

"Pick an apron," Gran said by way of greeting.

"Oh," Chase said, stopping in his tracks. "Okay." Chase picked up a light blue apron covered in white daisies. *Better than the one with teacups and lace around the edges.*

"Good choice. That was my mother's."

Chase smiled, putting on his great-grandmother's apron. *What is she up to?*

"I realized that I've had Chelsea and Sarah up to cook with me, but not you. So welcome to night one of Cooking Fun with Gran! D'ya like to cook?"

Chase smiled. "I can make scrambled eggs and tacos. Oh, and grits. Mom always has me make them when we're having them. You might say I'm famous for my grits."

Grinning, Gran grabbed out a pie plate and a bowl. "Good! Guess we're not startin' from scratch. We're gonna make us a pecan pie for dessert. But first things first. Pronunciation. What kind of pie are we making?"

"Pecan."

"Oh no." Gran shook her head. "A pee can is something you keep under your bed at night. It's pee-con."

"Gran, what on earth are you talking about?"

"My daddy told me, when there were outhouses, people would keep a container under their bed so they wouldn't have to go outside at night to pee. I ain't making a pie out of one of those pee cans!"

Chase couldn't stop laughing.

After they finished the pie, he and Gran made mac and cheese and biscuits to go with the food Gran had already prepared. Chase wasn't sure what his mom was going to find to eat that night that was healthy. *Maybe I should call her and tell her to eat a snack before coming. I'll eat her share.*

· · ● · ● · ● · · ·

After dinner, the family was sitting around the living room, talking about their lives and what was happening around town. As always, much of the conversation centered around people Chase didn't know. He kept one ear on the conversation, just in case, and one on his thoughts about his next art project. His art teacher wanted him to leave his beloved painting behind for this one. She'd challenged him to create a 3-D model using any material, and it had to be a representation of something extremely meaningful to Chase. He was thinking about his family and his friendship with Hershey when his aunt said his name.

"Chase," Aunt Cindy said. "Bring your magic hands over here. My shoulders and upper back are so tight today."

Chase, not being one to deny his elders, got up and went to his aunt. Her muscles did seem tight and he could feel several knots by her shoulder blades. Somehow, he had become his family's massage therapist. He knew once he was finished with his aunt, someone else would request to be next. *Does every family have a member with strong hands who gives out massages like candy at a parade?*

"Oh my gosh, that's so much better. I know you want to be an artist, but you should definitely consider this. Unless I'd have to start paying..."

Chase's phone rang in his pocket. He stopped massaging and pulled out his phone. *Linda Hershey—I wonder what she wants.*

"Hello?"

"Chase... there's been an accident. I know Chase would want you to be here." Mrs. Hershey sobbed. "Get here as soon as you can. He's in surgery now, but the doctor wasn't hopeful." As she spoke, her speech became more and more difficult to understand. Somewhere in the back of his mind, he wondered how she'd even managed to call him.

"Which hospital?"

"Park View."

"Okay. I'll be there soon."

As he hung up the phone, a wave of nausea crashed over Chase. He ran to the bathroom to be sick. *No. No. No. No. No. No. No. Not Hersh. No.*

Chase's dad drove him to the hospital. But by the time they got there, Hershey was gone.

16

Ruby

Age Eighteen

Ruby was called to the guidance office before calculus, where they gave her the news that she was going to be valedictorian. She couldn't wait to work on her speech. *It's going to be inspirational and funny. A "not a dry eye in the house" kind of speech.*

Ruby was writing speech ideas on the edge of her calculus notes when her teacher walked past her desk.

"Whatcha doin', Miss Butler?"

"Making notes, Mr. Wright." She gave him a guilty smile.

"Calculus involves more than I realized," her teacher said, glancing at her paper.

"I'll refocus," Ruby said, turning to a fresh sheet.

Not for the first time, She wished Vera hadn't moved. Mr. Wright had been their favorite teacher back when they were taking Algebra

II with him their freshman year. His dry sense of humor got them every time.

Vera had moved to New Hampshire toward the end of their sophomore year, but thankfully their friendship had been strong enough to survive the move. They chatted on the phone frequently and had each spent a week with the other during both summers. Most importantly, in less than five months they were moving to college as roommates. Ruby to pursue a degree in education to become a math teacher and Vera to find "some way I can get paid to do math things."

Ruby looked to her right at her boyfriend of six months, Ethan. He noticed her glance and gave her that crooked smile that had won her over to begin with. *I don't know that I'll ever get over that smile.* Ethan was going to college with them as well. Ruby was happy. Her future was bright.

After calculus, Ruby and Ethan headed to the cafeteria for lunch. She typically packed her lunch, but not on pizza Fridays. They went through the line and got their pizza, corn and apple, grabbed one of lunch lady Roberta's famous gooey chocolate chip cookies for an extra dollar and took their typical seats near their friends.

"I'm gonna have to go through the line again if I want to get enough to be full," Ethan said before eating half his pizza in two bites.

"Maybe you should start bringing a small lunch on pizza day to eat after your pizza, since this has become your traditional Friday comment," Ruby said between bites of corn.

"Maybe you're right, buttercup." Ethan booped her on the nose.

She rolled her eyes. "You're ridiculous. Let's face it, you're never going to find a pet name I'll be okay with."

"You know I'm not a quitter, pookie," Ethan beamed.

Ruby stared at him briefly, then turned to talk with the girl sitting on her other side.

Ethan grinned at her back and leaned over, kissed her cheek, then whispered into her ear, "I'll figure it out one day."

· · · · •·•· · · ·

That night, Ruby and her family were having a special dinner because Mamu was back after traveling for five months, her longest trip to date. She and Ethan were meeting for the first time. *I hope she likes him. But why wouldn't she? What's not to like? My parents love him. They may even love him more than they love me. Well, of course not, but it's probably closer than is usual for boyfriends and parents.*

Ruby was setting the table, waiting for their guests to arrive, when her mom walked into the dining room carrying a vase of flowers she had been arranging in the kitchen. "Your grandmother just called and said she's running a bit late. Good thing since we are too." Nichole laughed, setting the flowers in the center of the table. "When should Ethan be here?"

"Anytime, really. You know he never runs late."

As if on cue, the doorbell rang. Ruby looked at her mother and, posing like a magician, she said, "Ta-da!"

She danced over to the door. "Hello! Hello!" she called out, opening the door. Ethan stepped inside and gave her a bear hug. "Hello, jewel."

"Do I look like the singer of 'You Were Meant for Me'?"

Ethan choked out a laugh. "Twins. Identical." He walked toward Nichole and hugged her as well. "Thanks for having me, Mrs. Butler."

"Glad you're here, Ethan. Make yourself at home."

Charlie joined them in the living room, and he and Ethan greeted each other with a high five and a "Charlie, my main man" from Ethan. *They're so cute. If we end up getting married one day Charlie will get that brother he always complained I wasn't.*

The Butlers and Ethan enjoyed some appetizers while waiting on Mamu. As it turned out, she was only ten minutes late, arriving right as Jared was pulling the maple-glazed pork chops out of the oven. Everyone filled their plates, leaving introductions for the table, where Mamu sat across from Ethan.

"You must be Ethan," Mamu said, ignoring her food.

"Yes, ma'am. It's nice to meet you, Mrs. Butler," Ethan said, placing his napkin in his lap.

"You're welcome to call me Millie or Ms. Millie, if you'd rather."

"I'll do that." Ethan smiled, then took a bite of Nichole's supposedly famous bacon-pecan green beans. "These are delicious," he said toward Ruby's parents. "I've always thought green beans were kinda tasteless, but these are amazing."

"Thanks so much," Nichole said with a smile. "My mom always made bland green beans, so I set out to fix that."

"Mission accomplished," Ruby exclaimed.

Abruptly changing the subject, Mamu began her interrogation. "So, are you good enough for our Ruby?"

Ruby almost choked on her water.

"Mom, we already approve of him—this is not necessary," Jared admonished, eyes widening at his mother.

Ignoring her son and not giving Ethan a chance to respond, Mamu continued. "Do you realize how wonderful and special she is?"

"Mamu," Ruby said, making a *calm down* face.

"I do know how wonderfully special she is, and while I don't think I deserve her, I'm pretty sure no one does. I try my best to come close, though." Ethan smiled, taking everything in stride. *Good answer, sir.*

Mamu nodded. Seeming to accept this answer, she began eating.

After several moments of food-enjoying silence, Jared spoke. "So, Mom, tell us a little about your trip. I still can't believe how long you were gone."

"Yeah, we missed you, Mamu," Ruby added.

"Well, I missed you all too. I had a nice time, but I don't think we'll be taking another trip this long again. I wasn't enjoying it toward the end. Five months is too much for an old geezer like me."

"Old geezer." Nichole dramatically rolled her eyes. "Please."

Mamu laughed. "Well, I'm not as young as I once was."

"None of us are," Ethan added, shaking his head in mock seriousness.

Polite laughter surrounded them and then Mamu began telling them about her trip. She and the Collinses had traveled down the East Coast, west to Texas, then up and around the Midwest before heading back.

"You wouldn't believe how close you are to alligators in the Everglades. And the babies are so small. I wanted to touch one, but I also wanted to keep my hand. I'm not sure how protective the mothers are."

"I'm so glad you don't act on all the ideas you have," Jared murmured with a sigh.

· · · · ● · ● · · · ·

"Call me when you get home so I know you made it back safely," Ruby said, releasing Ethan from a nearly-five-minute swaying hug on the porch.

"I live ten minutes from here. You worry too much." Ethan chuckled and gave her one last little kiss before heading toward his car. "Of course I'll call you. I'll already be missing you." *Gosh, I love him.*

"I think I hear the neighbor making gagging noises," Ruby called from the porch, laughing.

Ethan got in his car and waved. She watched him pull away from her house, then went inside to wait for his call. Mamu was sitting on the big cushy chair in the living room. "One downside to RV life is there isn't room for chairs like this," she said as Ruby entered the room.

"This is the best chair," Ruby said, squeezing in with her grandmother. "It's my favorite spot to curl up and read." Ruby grabbed the throw from the basket by the chair. It was a chilly night for late April.

"I like Ethan," Mamu said, stroking Ruby's hair. "I'm not sure if he's the guy for you or not, but for now he'll do."

"We'll see." Ruby sighed, content.

17

Chase

THE PAIR DROVE FOR nearly half an hour, not really speaking, when suddenly the truck jolted.

"What in the world?" Ruby said, carefully hitting the brakes and steering the truck to the side of the road.

"I think a moose hit us," Chase said, eyes searching out the passenger-side window into the darkness.

"A moose hit *us*?"

"It happens."

"How would we know?"

"Maybe we should look for moose tracks," Chase said, turning back to Ruby, obviously suppressing a smile while eyeing the crumpled napkins from their ice cream cones.

She silently stared at him. *I'm pretty sure I saw her lip twitch.*

"I believe I saw a flash of moose antlers near my door," he added.

Ruby got out of the car and Chase tried to follow suit, but his door was jammed. He slid out the driver's side instead. They walked around the truck, and it certainly looked like it had been hit by a moose. The metal around the wheel well looked like a wadded-up piece of black paper. But the more pressing issue was that the tire was flat.

"How did that even happen?" asked Chase, kicking the tire in indication.

"Maybe the moose was carrying a knife?"

He turned to her and raised his eyebrows in disbelief. "She's got jokes," he said, laughing.

"That was obviously a serious suggestion," Ruby deadpanned.

"Obviously," he said gravely.

Ruby and Chase surveyed the damage for another minute before getting out the tools to change the tire. They worked together to remove the flat only to find the spare was flat as well. *Note to self, check the tire pressure of the spare before going to the trouble of changing the tire.*

"Crikey," Chase exclaimed under his breath.

"Crikey?"

"Oh. I've been watching a lot of old British television at night."

"Ah. Okay," Ruby said with a long exhale. "Now what? We haven't passed anything for at least twenty minutes and I don't have service. Do you?"

Chase reached into his pocket and grabbed his phone. "I do not. We were going what? Forty? So that means we haven't passed anything for maybe... thirteen miles?"

Ruby looked at him with a bit of surprise coloring her green eyes. "Oh. He's got math skills."

"I'm multifaceted," Chase said with a shrug and a smile. "I'd hate to be predictable."

· · · ● · ● · · ·

Chase and Ruby began walking south, the sun setting through the trees to their right. It was on the edge of being cool on this late June night. He had to slow his pace so she could keep up without a struggle.

"I'd like to paint that someday," Chase said mostly to himself as he looked toward the setting sun. The color was just right coming through the tree.

"You paint?"

"I do. I enjoy drawing as well, but painting is my thing, I suppose."

"What kinds of things do you paint? Real-life things, I suppose, since you mentioned the sunset?"

"Yeah, abstract isn't really my thing. I enjoy landscapes and portraits the most. I just finished one of my gran to give to her for her birthday."

"Is your grandmother anything like mine?"

"They're actually very similar. She taught me how to make pecan pie once and she has a very strong opinion on the pronunciation of *pecan*."

"And are you saying it like she does?" Ruby asked with an interested grin, kicking a rock down the street.

"Of course. She would somehow know if I wasn't."

"Pee-con. I'd argue against that just for fun, but I don't have a strong opinion. How was the pie?"

"Delicious, of course. She's a good cook. I miss her biscuits." Chase reached the rock Ruby had kicked a moment ago and gave it a kick himself.

Ruby's stomach growled. "Apart from the ice cream, when was the last time you ate anything?" she asked, jogging forward to kick the rock.

"I had some almonds and an apple shortly before I left for the bakery. You?"

"I had an egg sandwich at lunch, but then I got in the groove baking and never ate anything else. Of course, I'd assumed we would be back by eight or so and I would eat then."

"Maybe Ms. Millie has a stash in the truck somewhere."

"You never know with her. She'll either have nothing or the glove box will be filled to bursting with all manner of trash food."

"Trash food?"

"Yeah, you know, food that's tasty but has no nutritional value. Think cookies and chips."

"Well, maybe we'll come upon a convenience store where we can purchase our very own trash food. I want some sour cream and onion chips."

"Ooo yeah. And some pretzels!"

"Pretzels?" Chase stopped walking and stared at Ruby, shaking his head like she had lost her mind.

"Pretzels are good and if you think otherwise, you're wrong," Ruby replied, stopping as well.

"We're going to have to agree to disagree." Chase gave their rock another kick and moved on after it.

· · · ● · ● ● · · ·

"I'm thinking we should turn around," Ruby said with a bit of fear in her voice.

Is she afraid of the dark? That's unexpected. Chase shifted to walk just a bit closer to Ruby. "How long do you think we've walked? A couple miles?"

"I guess so. But who knows how long we might walk before we see anything? We should just wait by the truck for someone to drive by."

"I agree. And I'm hungry. We have to hold on to the hope of the glove box trash food."

Ruby's stomach growled again. "Oh, this is the worst!" she shouted, exasperated.

"Careful, we don't want to call more moose."

"Your face is a moose."

"Wow. My *face* is a moose?"

"I'm too tired and hungry to maintain my usual level of snappy comebacks."

She's so cute. Chase wished he could grab her hand for the walk back.

18

Ruby

THE DUO TURNED BACK toward the truck at a more leisurely pace than before, a comfortable silence settling around them like the fog that had begun to show in their path.

It was shortly after ten by the time Ruby and Chase made it back to the truck, which was unfortunately foodless, trash or otherwise. Ruby slid back her seat, took off her shoes and put her feet on the dash.

"Oh, my feet are throbbing. They're not used to a four-mile hike after working all day. You'd think my teacher feet would be fine."

"I'd be glad to rub them, if you'd like."

Ruby gave Chase an *are you crazy* face. "I think I'll pass, but thanks." He looked a little embarrassed to have offered. Maybe Ruby should have said yes, they hurt so much. *No. That's too much. Note to self, flats are not the shoes to be wearing when the need to walk four miles arises.*

"So you're a teacher?" Chase asked, taking off his own shoes. *I hope his feet don't stink.*

"Yeah. High school math. I teach Math I, II and III."

"I don't know what those are, but that's cool. I enjoyed math in general, but I really liked geometry."

"I can see that. There's certainly an art aspect to geometry that you probably picked up on."

"Definitely. So you enjoy it? Being a teacher."

"I do, yeah. It can be difficult because the age difference between me and my students is sometimes only seven years. Which causes problems at times, especially with some of the older boys."

"I bet it does," Chase said emphatically. "Oh man. That's awful. And awkward. Really awkward. I'm sorry you have to deal with that. Maybe you should slip back to middle school for a few years until you're old and less attractive."

"So in a matter of only a *few years*, I'll be old and less attractive? Thanks for that. Although," she said with a smirk, "it might make me less likely to be harassed by random masseurs."

Chase covered his face with his hands. "No, obviously not less attractive, but maybe to a teenager? And have I mentioned lately how sorry I am?"

"You haven't, but I think at this point I'm over it enough not to go full-blown mad massage customer on you again." Ruby yawned. "I'm so tired. Let's just sit and watch for a car. Don't wake me if I doze off." She gave a small laugh, settling in.

"Okey dokey."

"Okey dokey?" Ruby asked with raised eyebrows. "Never mind, we'll address that later."

· · · ● · ● · · · ·

Before Ruby knew it, Chase was asleep. *Well, that's not fair.* If she didn't have the exact right conditions, she'd never sleep. What a weird night it had been. She certainly hadn't woken up and thought, *I bet I'll get stranded in a car with Chase tonight.* He was actually a pretty interesting guy, but even if she could get past what had happened, Ruby was leaving before too long. Nothing could come of it. Plus, she still wasn't ready for anything serious.

Ruby was sitting facing the window, lost in her thoughts, when headlights flew past so quickly there was no time to react. *Well, there went our help for the night. Ugh.*

Chase suddenly started making noises. Ruby clicked on the truck's cabin light and saw that his face looked pained. He was moaning. "No. No. No," Chase mumble-yelled. *Should I wake him up? I guess so.*

"Chase, wake up."

No response apart from more moans and nos.

Ruby scooted closer to him. "Chase, you're dreaming." No response. She laid her hand on his arm. She could feel how tense he was. "Chase, wake up." The dream really had a hold on him. Ruby noticed Chase's troubled face seemed to shimmer. Sweat.

She turned, grabbed his shoulders and lightly shook him. "Chase, wake up, you're dreaming." His eyes flew open and he reached his arms around Ruby's waist, tugging her closer. She could feel his heart pounding and the wild force of his breathing. *The circumstances of this hug aren't great, but this feels so good. So cozy and warm. He's strong.*

"Whatever was happening in your dream wasn't real. You're here with me, unsuccessfully waiting to be rescued." His breathing slowed and she could feel him relaxing. He seemed to realize they were hugging and released her.

"I'm sorry, I..."

"Needed comfort."

"Yeah, I guess so." A single tear slid down his cheek. Resisting the sudden urge to wipe away his tear, Ruby moved back to the middle of the bench seat and rubbed his upper arm and shoulder.

"I'm sorry if I woke you," Chase said when he had gathered himself enough to speak again.

"I was definitely not asleep," Ruby said with a half smile. "And even if you had, it's not like you did it on purpose." She realized she was still rubbing his arm and it was probably well past time to stop. *Feels nice, though.* She removed her hand and continued. "Do you want to talk about it?"

"I mean, there's really no need," Chase said, still adjusting to being awake and not trapped within a nightmare. "It's a recurring nightmare I have. And actually I've been having it less and less frequently the past couple years." Chase dropped his head back against the headrest, closing his eyes.

"Well, that's positive. I wonder what triggered it tonight."

"I was just wondering the same," Chase said, turning his head to look at Ruby. "My best friend, Hershey, died in a car crash our senior year of high school, and this dream about his death has haunted me ever since." Chase almost whispered the last part, and Ruby saw fresh tears in his eyes. "I've never really noticed a trigger, but in my dream I'm always in a car. The only part of the dream that varies is the beginning. This time, I was driving and I looked in the right lane and there was a fox wearing a top hat riding a motorcycle. I was doing my best to take a picture, but I was driving and couldn't get one safely. The next thing I know, I was stopped at an intersection and I witnessed Hershey's car crash and I saw him. He was reaching for me, but I couldn't get out of the car to get to him. The car has me trapped to watch him die."

"Oh my gosh, Chase, what a horrifying thing to dream," Ruby whispered, scooting over next to him, stretching up to put an arm around his shoulders. *Well, this is an unexpected turn of events. Why am I touching him again?*

Chase turned his head to look at her, putting their faces only inches apart. Ruby stared into his stormy blue eyes and saw the shadow of his pain. The ache in his heart not yet washed away by time or whatever it was that he needed. His face tugged at her heart a bit more than she was comfortable with, so she broke eye contact, removed her arm from his shoulders and stared unseeing out the windshield.

"Do you find it difficult having a dog named after him? Wouldn't it be a constant reminder?"

"Not really. It helps me keep a fun little piece of him without having to think too hard about it and going too far into my thoughts and feelings. He was like a brother, so I've had quite a journey through mourning and acceptance."

In that moment, Ruby realized she had forgiven Chase, but she knew she could go no further than forgiveness. No feelings, not even friendly ones. *I don't live here. My family isn't here, apart from Mamu, and I don't want to move. Plus, what a terrible story about how we met. I can't imagine telling that particular gem to anyone.*

Chase cleared his throat. "Well, that was all very heavy. How would you feel about playing a game?"

"A game?"

"Yeah, two truths and a lie?"

"Well, what else is there? Sure. You first."

"Okay." Chase squinted his eyes and tapped his chin with his finger, feigning deep, serious thought. "Alright, I got it. One, I play the guitar. Two, I won a local hot dog eating contest the year I moved here. Three, when I was a child, I got hit in the head with a golf club and my mom superglued my scalp together."

"Wow, there's really a lot there. Let's see. I think you do play the guitar because that one was less detailed, so I'm betting you didn't make it up. Now that leaves the other two." Ruby mimicked Chase's previous thinking face. "The golf club one seems like one you wouldn't make up on the spot. So that means the hot dog eating contest is the lie!" She yelled her guess, pointing at him, confident in her victory.

"Sherlock, that was a little loud for the confines of the truck. But you aaaaaare correct!"

"I knew it! You're not the hot dog eating contest kind of guy."

"What kind of guy is that, exactly?"

Ruby laughed. "I don't know. I was going to say someone with a huge belly, but that's not necessarily true."

"So, you've noticed I don't have a huge belly? I'm immensely flattered."

"Oh, hush. It's my turn. Let's see." She mimicked the thinking face again. "Okay. One, I love reading cookbooks but hardly ever use them. Two, I hate cheap flip-flops. Three, in middle school, I fell down a flight of stairs and was so embarrassed that I ran straight out the door, leaving school in the middle of the day."

Chase raised his eyebrows at number three. "I feel like you're trying to trick me."

Ruby smirked. *Of course I am.*

"Hmmm... I'm going to reverse your logic and say that you don't actually hate cheap flip-flops."

"Wrong. Cheap flip-flops are the worst."

"But you don't have to worry about ruining them."

"Believe it or not, I don't typically ruin my shoes anymore."

"Okay, okay. I'm wrong. But let me guess from the remaining two."

"Fine. But let the record show that I won this round."

"Yeah, yeah. Let me think." Chase furrowed his brow and pretended to repeatedly stroke a massive beard.

That's hilarious. Ruby suppressed the urge to laugh. She didn't want to let him know how funny she found him. She gave a small smile. She couldn't help it.

"I think you didn't fall down the stairs in middle school."

"Oh yeah?"

"Yeah," Chase proclaimed with a cocky tilt to his head.

"What makes you so sure?"

"I think you might be the type to get embarrassed, but not the type to break the rules and leave. Also, I'm just guessing here, but I think you were probably a bit of a nerd and you wouldn't have wanted to leave school."

How is he so right?!

"Maybe you meant that nerd part as an insult, but I take it as a compliment. Nerds are the best."

"So you're saying I'm the best?" Chase asked with a cocky grin.

"Your mom probably thinks so," Ruby said with an equally cocky grin.

"So does your mom."

"Ewwwww!"

"No! No," Chase half-yelled, dodging their napkin trash flying his way. "I meant your mom thinks I'm the best instead of you."

"I'll choose to believe you, because I'm not lingering on this."

"Good. So I was right?"

"Yes, you were. I think I have a cookbook problem."

"Yes! So do you cook, just without a cookbook?"

"I love baking. That's why I offered to come help Mamu. But regular cooking? I do the basics to get by, but I really don't enjoy it. I get the cookbooks thinking I'll get inspired, but I never do."

"How many do you have?"

"I probably have five right now, but who knows how many I've donated. How about you? Do you cook?"

"I actually do, yeah. I don't know that my cooking is anything special, but my gran taught me quite a bit in addition to that pecan pie in the few years before I moved here."

"What's your specialty?"

"I make delicious grits. So maybe breakfast?"

"Grits! I thought you had a southern accent. I've never had grits."

"Oh, bless your heart," Chase laughed. "Yes, I'm from North Carolina. I moved here—"

KNOCK. KNOCK. KNOCK.

Chase and Ruby both jumped. *Holy guacamole!* Somehow they had missed a vehicle pulling up behind them. Two people were silhouetted standing outside the driver's window, shining flashlights in on them.

"Ruby, honey, it's Mamu and Gerald."

"Oh!" Ruby sighed. She rolled down the window, turning to Chase. "I thought that murderer she was worried about had finally shown up."

"I'm so glad we found you. When you never came back I got so worried."

"Worried," Gerald said, then added, "she was frantic."

Ruby and Chase got out of the truck. "Sorry about the moose damage, Mamu."

"Eh. That's what insurance is for, honey. I'm just glad you guys are alright."

19

Chase

AGE TWENTY

CHASE HAD SPENT THE better part of the last two years mourning Hershey and the future they had planned. He didn't go to college. Had barely been able to finish high school. Chase had been living at home, doing odd jobs as a learn-as-you-go handyman.

He walked around in a near-constant state of melancholy, isolating himself from anyone or anything that would bring him joy. Knowing he would never get close with anyone again. People die and then there's just you left with a haunting absence and bittersweet memories. Why would he want to risk going through that again?

One morning, while on his bed staring at the ceiling, a thought hit Chase. *I need to get out of here.* So much of their town reminded him of Hershey. He had a small fear that if he left, he would forget about his friend, lose the memories that were all he had left of him. Deep down, however, he knew he had those memories locked in. He just needed not to be constantly reminded of them. *I know I will never have another friend like him. I'll pour myself into my art and that will be enough for me.*

The alarm on his phone chimed. He didn't know why he set an alarm anymore. He always woke around five, fell too deep into his feelings and was then unable to go back to sleep. Here it was seven in the morning, time for him to get ready for his standing appointment with Mrs. Powers from down the street. *I wonder what she has for me today. I hope nothing to do with that terrible cat of hers. I don't think my scratches have healed from last week.* Chase looked down and sure enough, the pink scratches were still marring his forearm.

"Thanks, Stella."

• • • • ● • ● • • • •

"Chase, dear, come in," Mrs. Powers said, opening her front door. "Have some coffee and I'll tell you what we're doing today." Mrs. Powers, who was originally from Charleston, had the most beautiful accent.

"Oh, no, thank you. I had some at the house before I came." Mrs. Powers made the worst coffee. *I don't need to grow chest hair on the inside.*

"I insist," she said, filling her biggest mug for him. "We've got a big day today. I want white cabinets. These old yellow-brown things have got to go. I told Bert that for years, but he never got around to it." Bert and Ann Powers had lived down the street from Chase and his family since Chase was three. Mr. Powers, a man without a single handyman bone in his body, had passed six months ago, leaving Mrs. Powers in a less-than-ideal living situation. Chase had been helping her fix things every Monday for the past five months. Today, however, was a want rather than a need. *A nice change of pace for Mrs. Powers. I bet it's better to cook in a kitchen you actually like.* He had been the recipient of many sweet treats from that kitchen. As good as she was at baking, he always found it hard to believe that she couldn't get coffee figured out.

Chase choked on his first sip.

· · · ● · ● · · · ·

After a day of sanding and painting, Chase was spent. He had worked hard, especially during the last half of the day. He wanted to make sure he didn't leave Mrs. Powers in a mess for the next week. Still, he was only half-finished and he insisted on going back the next day to attach the ones that were drying overnight.

I need a coffee—a professionally made coffee. Chase was ready to research and plan. He wanted to figure out his life moving forward and go.

Chase walked to his house to grab his laptop, calling out when he stepped inside. "Hey, Mom, I'm going to get coffee. Need anything?"

"If you're going to Beans & Brews, will you see if they have any gluten-free muffins?"

Chase's mom had celiac disease and could never get her gluten-free baking to have anything close to a normal texture. Beans & Brews didn't have that problem.

"Sure, Mom. If they do, how many do you want?"

"I want two dozen, but how about just two?"

"Sure thing." *I'm gonna get her four.* "I'll be home by six."

. . . .

It had only been a few months since he had been able to go back into Beans & Brews. In high school, it was his and Hershey's favorite after-school spot to sit and maybe do homework. It was by far the best coffee shop in the area, so he'd eventually gathered the courage to go back. The memories still hit him each time he walked in the door, but they were starting to dissipate. Or at least they seemed to be turning less bitter and more sweet.

As he walked in, he saw that Lacey was working. *I'm too tired to deal with her and her flirting.*

Chase sighed and approached the counter.

"Chase! Hey! Long time no see. Where have you been, handsome?"

Lacey had gone to school with Chase. She was a nice and pretty girl with chocolate-brown hair, and apparently she couldn't take a hint.

"I've been in a few times lately when you weren't working."

"Maybe I need to give you a copy of my schedule," Lacey said, leaning forward and batting her eyelashes a bit too aggressively.

Can't you see that I'm emotionally unavailable and would make an awful boyfriend? "Isn't the mystery more exciting?" *Why on earth did I say that? That sounded like flirting.*

"Maybe so," Lacey said, smiling, then noticing the line building behind Chase. "What can I get for you today?"

Your realization that this won't be happening and "An americano." He took a breath, considering. "You know what, actually, I'll have a mocha with whipped cream and four gluten-free cinnamon swirl muffins."

"I didn't know you're gluten-free."

"I'm not, but my mom is."

"That's so sweet of you to get these for her," Lacey said with adoring eyes.

Chase gave her a small smile and stepped out of the way for the next customer. When he received his order, he sat at a table near the window, which happened to be as far as he could get from the register. Chase powered up his obnoxiously slow laptop and began his research.

· · · ● · ● · · · ·

By the time Chase needed to leave to get home for dinner, he had a rough plan. He decided to rip off the band-aid, so to speak, and tell his parents at dinner. He followed the scent of chicken pie to the dining room and filled his plate before beginning.

"I've been thinking that I need a change," Chase began, taking a bite of his salad. *I hope Mom doesn't freak out or get sad.* "I need to move away, at least for a while."

"Oh... oh, okay," replied his mom, surprised. "What has led you to this decision?"

"I think it will help me move on and hopefully finally recover from losing Hershey. There's just so much of him here. Hopefully I can move back one day and be able to enjoy the memories." As he spoke,

Chase watched his mother's face go from slight panic to peaceful understanding.

"I think this could be really good for you, Chase. Sometimes you have to take big steps or even leaps to change your life."

"I agree, son." His dad reached over and squeezed his arm. "Do you know where you'd like to go?"

"One of my favorite artists, Ryan Kishlar, lives in a small town in Maine. I was thinking I might go there, get a job and try to meet him. See if he'll take me under his wing for a bit. That part might be a long shot, but I reckon it's worth a try."

"Didn't you tell me that he's a recluse?" his dad asked before shoveling in a huge bite of chicken pie.

"I believe he's known to be a nice man who is a *bit* of a recluse."

"What will you do for a job?" Chase's mother asked, concern beginning to show on her face once again.

"There's a massage therapy school not far from here and I can be certified in six months. I found there are two spas not terribly far from where Mr. Kishlar is. My hope is I can get a place with one of them. I'm going to contact them and see if it's a possibility."

"You do have magic hands," his mother commented with a smile.

"That sounds like a good plan," Chase's father added. "You know we're here to support you in any way we can, right? We'll miss you terribly, but we want you to be happy."

Chase sighed with relief. "Thanks, Dad. I know. And I'll let you know what I hear from the spas and keep you updated, of course. I'm trying to get on this soon because I would need to start school in three weeks."

After dinner, Chase helped his dad with the dishes and then they all enjoyed an episode of *Seinfeld* before he went to bed. He fell asleep hard and fast, sleeping better than he had in two years, not waking until his alarm went off the next morning.

20

Ruby

Age Twenty-Two

By senior year, Ruby and Vera had moved to an off-campus apartment with two girlfriends they had met along the way. Ruby was well on her way to graduating this spring with a degree in secondary education and a minor in math. Vera had decided on engineering during their sophomore year and would finish up after an extra semester next fall.

Ruby was in their living room, reading for pleasure, for once, when she paused and looked at her setup. *I think I might be too bougie to be a teacher.* She took in her smart wool socks and continually warming coffee mug. *I might just have to make very specific Christmas lists and hope for the best.*

"Ruuuuuby!" Vera burst into the room and dropped her bag by the door. "I am so over this semester. If I have to write another lab report, I might burst into flames." Vera plopped down on the sofa next to Lucy.

"Rough day?" Ruby asked, offering her coffee cup to Vera, who accepted the cup with a nod.

"I'm just tired and sick of having to work so hard. Things seem to come so easily to so many of my classmates, but I have to work for it. I just need something easy for once. Blech."

"Oh, Vera, I'm sorry. I know that's really frustrating." She didn't really understand. She loved her classes and had thrived knowing she was right where she needed to be.

"Don't get me wrong, it's interesting and sometimes fun, but more often, it's just too much." She gave Ruby back her now-empty cup and dropped her head to the back of the sofa.

"Let's do something fun tonight. We could go to that Thai place you love and go see a movie." Ruby laid her head on her friend's shoulder.

"That sounds amazing. Yes, sign me up." She took a deep and slow breath. "Are we inviting the boyfriends?"

"Up to you!"

"I say yeah, let's invite them. I'm gonna go call Brady."

"Sounds good, I'll call Ethan and we'll reconvene."

Vera headed to her room and Ruby picked up her phone and called Ethan. The call went straight to voicemail. She knew he wasn't in class. Ruby got up, washed her cup and went to her room to get ready. She tried him a second time and when it went to voice mail again, she decided she would go find him.

"Vera," she called down the hall. "I'm going to run over to Ethan's. I think his phone is dead or something. I'll meet you at the restaurant at six, with or without Ethan, okay?"

"Okay, see you there!"

· · · ● · ● · · · ·

Ruby climbed the stairs to Ethan's apartment and found the door unlocked. She called out, but there was no answer. Loud music was streaming out of Ethan's room.

"Hey you," she called out as she stepped into his doorway. Ethan jumped up and away from the disheveled blond on his bed.

Ruby couldn't speak. Couldn't move. Her boyfriend of nearly five years had been on his bed making out with another girl. *I might vomit.*

"Ruby! What are you doing here? I... ummm...," Ethan said, looking from Ruby to the girl.

"Ethan, who is this?" the girl asked.

The audacity.

Ruby recovered her speech. "Who am I? I'm his girlfriend. Who are you?!"

The girl glared daggers at Ethan. "So you made me the 'other woman'? What is wrong with you?"

So she's innocent, I guess. I still think I hate her a little bit.

"Ashley, it's been over with her for a while. I just hadn't officially broken it off."

"Don't call me, Ethan," Ashley said as she got up and left the room.

"It's been over for a while, has it? Do tell, when did we end? I somehow missed that."

"Teddy bear, I just said that to make her feel better. I'm so sorry. She came here to study and next thing I knew she was all over me."

"How dare you. Your stupid pet names didn't work when you were being loving to me. They sure aren't helpful now!" Ruby gave him a look of pure disgust. She continued, "Do you often have girls over to study on your bed?"

"No, but Mike and his friend were out there playing video games when we started."

"So where are your study materials?"

Ethan looked around and, of course, there wasn't a book in sight.

Instead of giving him a chance to tell more lies, she spoke again. "I can honestly say I have never been more shocked in my entire life. I just knew we were going to be getting married before too long." Ruby was beginning to lose the battle of fighting back tears.

"Ruby, I love you," Ethan declared, taking a step towards her. She raised a hand, silently telling him to stop.

"No, you don't. Or maybe you do, but it doesn't matter now. You know what, as much as this hurts, I'm glad you did it now instead of waiting until we were married. It's much easier to deal with a cheating boyfriend."

"No. You don't need to deal with me. This will never happen again, you have my word."

"Your word means nothing. Please pack anything you have of mine. I'll be waiting by the stairs." Ruby turned and left, ignoring his begging cries.

· · · · ● · ● · · · ·

Ethan brought Ruby a box of her things, tears in his eyes and lies in his mouth. She told him he could pick up his junk from her doorstep tomorrow. She texted Vera when she got to her car and asked her to cancel with Brady and stay put. Thankfully, she had been solidly composed as she was driving, but as soon as she put the car in park outside the apartment, a wave of nausea hit her. Ruby put her head on the steering wheel, feeling like her world had just flipped upside down.

Moments later there was a light tap on her window. *If Ethan has followed me here, I swear...* She looked up and Vera was there. Ruby opened her door and was immediately embraced by her friend. Vera helped Ruby out of her car, then put her arm around her shoulders and they walked to their apartment, where Ruby told her everything that had happened.

"That monster. I'll slash his tires."

"No, you won't." Ruby gave her friend a weak smile.

"Of course not, but only because I don't want to get caught. I'm so mad."

"I guess I'm mad, but I'm mostly hurt, I think," Ruby said, hugging a pillow to her chest. "Hurt and shocked. I would never have thought him the type."

Vera sighed and shook her head. "You know what, we need to get out of here. Would your parents be up for a weekend visit from both of us? My second class is canceled tomorrow, so I'm finished at nine thirty."

"You're absolutely right. I'm sure they're up for it, but I'll double-check. Great idea." Ruby got up, dropped her alpaca throw on the sofa and headed toward her room. "I'm going to give them a call and pack up Ethan's trash. I hope somebody steals it before he gets over here."

"That's the spirit!" Vera laughed.

· · · ● · ● · · · ·

The girls got to Ruby's family home early Friday afternoon. They pulled into the driveway to find Mamu's RV parked there and Mamu sitting in a rocking chair on the porch.

"My darling girls, you're here!" Mamu called, walking down the porch steps.

"Hi, Mamu," they said in unison and laughed.

She group hugged them and took Ruby's hand, leading them toward the door. "I've got news, and you guys are going to be the first to know!" Mamu's grin was like the Cheshire cat's and she seemed more bubbly than usual. *What is she up to?*

They went into the kitchen and poured themselves some tea. "Extra lemon in mine, please," Mamu said, taking a seat at the kitchen table. Despite the fact that she was obviously bursting at the seams to tell them her news, she checked in on them first. "So how are you girls? How's school?"

"We've got some stuff, but I don't personally want to talk about it right now," Ruby said. "I want to hear about your news." Vera nodded her agreement.

"Okay! You know my second cousin Shirley? Well, you wouldn't, Vera, but trust me, I do have a second cousin named Shirley. Anywho, she has owned a bakery in Maine for the past fifteen years and she's ready to give it up. She wants the business to stay in the family, and when she told me, I just knew it was for me."

"You're moving to Maine?!" Ruby asked, surprised. "I thought you were still loving the RV life."

"I still plan to live in the RV. I'm just comfortable there, ya know? There's an apartment above the bakery, which I plan to rent out."

"Maine isn't close enough for me," Ruby pouted, pushing out her bottom lip for dramatic effect.

"I know, honey. It's just over five hours from here. You can come for visits and I'll come back too. Promise. But also, they've got high schools and engineering needs in Maine too." Mamu wiggled her eyebrows at the girls. "I'm just sayin'."

21

Chase couldn't get Ruby off his mind. The feeling of her in his arms. How right it had felt. Once he'd realized what he was doing, he'd held on to her a moment longer. He couldn't help it. He had felt like he had found something he had been missing. It wasn't just the contact, it was something else. Something about Ruby. He hadn't needed her comfort by the end, but he wanted it. Wanted her. He couldn't help but notice that she touched him quite a bit. More than he thought necessary. He had savored her touch like the last bites of something delicious.

Chase had the day off and not quite enough to do to distract himself from his thoughts of Ruby and the near-constant replay of the events of last night. He was used to being able to leave little attractions behind, but then perhaps this wasn't such a little attraction.

He wondered how he could manage to get another hug the next time he saw her. *Fake a nightmare?*

He laughed at himself. "Okay, Chase," he said to the empty room. "Calm down and figure out your day." At the sound of his voice, Tuck and Hershey bounded into the room.

"Ah, boys, what are we doing today?" Chase sat on the floor and gave them both belly rubs. "Did you say you'd like to go for a run? You did, didn't you? Alright, go get ready, I need to find my shoes."

Chase found his running shoes in a yet-to-be-unpacked box sitting by his closet door. He got the dogs on their leashes and they headed out. The day was unseasonably warm, which he loved, and the sun was bright, energizing Chase, inspiring a quicker-than-normal run. When he reached a crossroad, he had a decision to make. He could turn left toward some of his favorite trails, or right toward town. *Town feels right for today.* He didn't admit to himself the motivation behind that feeling.

As he drew closer to town, he spotted a runner ahead of him. He knew exactly who it was—Ainsley Balf, the second woman he'd tried to casually date when he'd moved here. She had not reacted well to being put off, and while he wouldn't consider her a stalker, he wouldn't put her far off the mark either. Chase slowed his pace so he wouldn't catch up with her, but she stopped, taking a seat on a bench and answering her phone. He considered taking another route but thought he would speed up instead and fly past her without notice. After all, he was on the exact route he wanted to be on.

As Chase approached at high speeds, Ainsley took her phone from her ear and looked up. "Chase!" she called out with a huge smile. He groaned internally and slowed. What convenient timing to end her phone call... *I should have just taken the long way around. Would it have really hurt?*

"Hey, Ainsley. How are you doing?" When he stopped, Tuck jumped up onto Ainsley, who made an ooof sound, then laughed in such a way that he knew she didn't like it but was trying to seem like everything was fine.

"I'm doing well. Haven't seen you in a while. How've you been?" Ainsley stood, putting herself, of course, much too close to Chase.

"I'm well. Busy, though." *Let me plant that nugget for when I escape in thirty seconds.*

"Busy doing what? Looks like you've been exercising that fine body of yours," Ainsley said, reaching for his arm.

He rotated a bit to avoid her touch. "Well, that's what I'm doing now, so I guess so. Speaking of, I'm trying to keep my heart rate up, so I better get going."

"So, soon?"

"Yeah, it's almost back to normal now."

"Okay, then, see you around."

"Bye, Ainsley."

"Oh, Chase!" she called after him. *I knew that was too easy.*

"Yeah?" he asked, turning.

"Are you going to the dance?"

"I'm not sure." Chase held up his hand to her and turned, running nearly as fast as he could. *What have I done? What if she bids on me?* He hadn't thought things through well enough when Mrs. Maxwell roped him into auctioning himself. *What am I going to do? I wonder if she would put a caveat below my item, something like "no one I have previously dated may bid." That could work.*

Chase saw the sign for The Sweet Spot Bakery in the distance. He slowed his pace to give himself more time in the vicinity of the bakery, for some reason. As he and the dogs approached the bakery window, he slowed to barely a jog, looking inside. He didn't see anyone, not that he was looking for anyone in particular. *Stop it. Now* you're *being a stalker.*

He was picking up the pace when someone rounded the corner of the bakery, nearly colliding with Hershey. Chase looked up to see Gerald. "Going somewhere in a hurry?" Gerald smiled, bending to pet Chase's dogs.

Chase laughed. "I always have time for you, Mr. Jones."

"As it turns out, I don't have time for *you* today. I'm taking Millie out on a special date tonight and I have to get it set up."

"Must be quite the setup to be starting at ten in the morning."

"When they're worth it, they're worth it." Gerald smiled, shrugging. "Stop into the shop, I've got the book you loaned me sitting by the cash register."

"Thanks! I'll have to come back another time, though. I'm not sure your other customers would appreciate my current stink."

"You know what, I appreciate that. I don't smell you, but you do look like you got in a shower with your clothes on."

Chase plucked at his shirt sticking to his torso. "It's hot out this morning and I might have pushed it a little too hard today during parts of my run. The dogs are grateful, though, I think."

"Probably so," Gerald replied with a chuckle. "I'll see ya later on, Chase."

"Bye, Mr. Jones, enjoy your date!" Chase said as Gerald walked away.

Feeling, for some reason, disappointed with his run, Chase headed home.

22

Ruby

"Mamu, that apple pie is gorgeous. Have you ever thought of starting an Instagram page? This would make a beautiful post. We could save the photo for an Independence Day post and say something like 'American as apple pie,'" Ruby suggested while admiring her grandmother's latest creation.

"Thank you, sweetheart, I think a lattice crust always looks nice." Mamu grabbed a box for the pie, adding, "I'm not really a fan of the social media." She started placing the pie in the box, but Ruby stopped her.

"Just let me take a photo, in case we want to use it one day."

Ruby set the pie on the butcher block counter near the window and snapped a simple photo. "Maybe I can set up a page for you. Just for especially pretty items. Or if you wanted to advertise specials like yours and Gerald's idea."

"I'd be glad for you to do that, honey, but I'm not sure who will take care of it when you're gone."

"We'll figure it out." Ruby smiled warmly while boxing up the pie.

"Would you mind taking this to Chase? I made it to thank him for helping you get the picnic table for me. Apple pie is his favorite."

"Do I get a pie?" Ruby asked with raised eyebrows.

"You can ask him for a slice when you take it," Mamu stated matter-of-factly through what Ruby was sure was a held-in smile.

She thinks she's so clever.

"But my favorite is French silk." Ruby lifted her chin and placed her hands on her hips like a righteous, petulant child.

"That's good to know, dear." Mamu patted Ruby's arm and headed toward her RV.

· · • • · • • • · ·

Later that afternoon, Ruby drove over to Chase's house. As she was walking to the door, a noise from the backyard caught her attention and she turned that way. Chase was there, chopping wood, wearing headphones and *not* wearing a shirt. Ruby was frozen to her spot. *Holy guacamole. Look at those back muscles.* His sweat accentuated the divets and curves of his powerful back. Chase lifted the ax again and Ruby knew she would have stumbled had she not been standing still. *Was Vera right? Am I into lumberjacks?!* He turned and caught her staring.

Oh no.

Chase had turned to add a log to his pile when he saw her. Ruby felt her face turn scarlet and was grateful she wasn't terribly close to him. Which was something she had not been grateful for only a moment ago.

Chase slammed his ax into a piece of wood and headed her way, removing his headphones. The sun was shining on him in just the right way as he walked to her in what Ruby perceived as dramatic slow motion. She thought she might faint. *I didn't know masseur boys could look like this. Ruby, no feelings, no attraction. Guys aren't trustworthy. I'm leaving at the end of summer. Am I still red?*

"Hey, Bee," Chase said with an easy smile.

"Hi." *Why was that the squeakiest thing I have ever said?!*

Ruby cleared her throat and tried again. "Hey, sorry, I think the heat is getting to me. I didn't think it got this hot in Maine, although we're really not that much farther north than where I live in southern Vermont. I'm thinking I shouldn't have showered this morning. Waste of time." *Stop talking, Ruby.* "Maybe it's a heat wave. I'm so thankful the bakery has AC. Oh, that's right, you lived there. You know about the AC."

By the end of her monologue, Chase was looking at her with slightly raised eyebrows. "Yes, I remember the AC quite well. I could always tell when Ms. Millie was making cinnamon rolls."

Ruby gave the most awkward chuckle possible and pretended to study the logs and fallen tree. *Get yourself together right now. Is a gorgeous, shirtless, shining man standing less than two feet from me? Yes. Do I have to turn into a bumbling idiot? Probably not.*

"This tree fell during the storm the other day. I thought I'd prep some firewood for the winter. I've never had a wood-burning fireplace."

Ruby looked back at him, nodding. *What did he say? I was so focused on my idiocy and not staring at him that I missed it.* She decided to change the subject and hope for the best, but her useless brain was emptier than it had ever been. *Think, Ruby, your brain still works!*

"Eyes up here, please," Chase said with a smirk.

"Oh! Oh, sorry. I wasn't staring, I was just lost in thought."

"About?"

"You know. Stuff and things." *Stuff and things? What is wrong with me?*

"That does sound like something important to think about right now."

They stood in silence for a moment before Ruby blurted, "Would you like to put on a shirt?"

"Is my skin offending you?"

"Why wouldn't it?"

"You're right. I can see why you'd be bothered." *Oh, I'm bothered alright.* Chase made a bit of a show of stretching his ax-wielding muscles, then waved her toward the house. "Come on in and I can save your delicate eyes."

Chase led Ruby in through the side entrance, which was not where she had entered the house the previous night. She stepped into a huge screened porch and saw that it was set up as a painting studio.

"Do you have a roommate?" Ruby asked, setting the pie on a table and crouching to pet Hershey and Tuck, who had been lounging on the porch. She stood to find Chase, still shirtless, standing well within her personal space. She took in a sharp breath. *He doesn't even stink. What is this sorcery?*

"Nope, no roommate," Chase said, heading to the door leading to the main part of the house. "Feel free to look around. I'm gonna go grab a shirt."

I'm rethinking that rather rash request.

"Okay."

Chase left and Ruby sauntered around the room, taking in the sights. He had two completed paintings leaning against the wall. One was a breathtaking forest scene, perhaps in the morning or nearing sunset? The other was an absolutely stunning portrait of an older woman. *Oh yeah, he did that painting of his grandmother—guess this is it.*

As she took in the paintings around the room, she realized that not only was Chase an artist, he was a legitimate, spectacular artist. *I can't believe he hasn't casually dropped this into conversation. "Oh, by the way, I make paintings that could sell for thousands. No big deal."*

Ruby turned and began looking at the painting on the easel. Chase had clearly just started it. The colors looked like the beginning of a sunset. She knew when it was finished, it would rival anything she had seen in the actual sky.

Chase returned and joined Ruby at the easel. "That's the sunset from last night," he said, straightening some items on his painting table. "The hues coming through the trees were calling to me, so I thought I would try to recreate it." He smiled and shrugged. *Could he be any more attractive? Good grief.*

"It was a beautiful night, although I can't say that I paid any particular attention to it. I was too busy being stressed about our situation." Ruby looked at the paints on the table and ached to pick up a brush and try her hand. She had never had any real skill in any form of art, but she had always enjoyed painting for fun.

Ruby turned to face the paintings against the wall and Chase stepped to look over her shoulder, crowding into her space once again. "Who is this lovely lady? Your grandmother?"

Chase stepped around Ruby and picked up the painting. "This is my gran. She turns seventy-five in September, so I'm going home for her birthday and giving this to her. Do you think it would be weird to get a painting of yourself? I didn't think about that until I was finished."

"I don't think so. Especially if it's from your grandson." The pair stood taking in the painting and Ruby noticed Chase had his grandmother's storm cloud–blue eyes.

"She'll love it," she added, turning to him and smiling.

He smiled brightly and returned the painting to its post against the wall. "Thanks, Bee."

Bee. He called me that earlier. I think I like it.

23

Chase

She is precious. She's like a baby bird I want to hold in my hands, nourish and protect. Although, I think she might be a falcon. Those need nourishing and protecting sometimes too, right? I could like her. No, I could love her. Was he ready to risk that kind of loss? He already knew she would be leaving.

Chase stepped away and towards the pie. "I assume this is the reason you stopped by," he said with a wide grin.

"Oh. Yes, Mamu baked this for you as a thank-you for helping to pick up the picnic table," Ruby answered, walking toward him.

"Apple pie!" Chase enthusiastically opened the box. "She's the best. What kind did you get?"

"A little-known pie called 'thank you and hug pie.' It's delicious. You should be very jealous," Ruby deadpanned.

"Well, I'll share some of mine, if you share some of yours."

"Thank you."

"You're right. That was delicious. Do I get a portion of the hug too?" *There's a way I could relive that portion of last night.*

"You'll have to take that up with her." *Well, it was worth a shot.*

"I might just do that. Come on to the kitchen." Chase waved her on and she followed behind him.

"I don't have any ice cream," he said as if delivering seriously bad news. "But if you can wait just a few minutes, I can make some whipped cream."

"You make whipped cream?"

"You don't live above a bakery for three years and learn nothing," Chase said, placing his mixing bowl and beater into the freezer. "Sometimes I put it in my coffee. Or on pancakes. OH! Did you know you can freeze dollops and put them in hot chocolate? I did that for my parents last year when we went to look at Christmas lights on Christmas Eve."

"You've developed a real passion for whipped cream, eh?"

"It's just below painting and just above... everything else," Chase said with feigned sincerity.

Ruby gave a reluctant smile.

I like her smile. I'd like to see more of it.

"How old are you? I'm assuming it's not rude to ask, if you believe the person is around your age." He crossed to the panty to retrieve the sugar, smiling at Ruby.

"I'm ninety-five, you?"

"I was right, we are close. I'm ninety-three."

She smiled and just like before, Chase took it and tucked it in his heart.

"I'm actually twenty-five."

"And *I'm* actually only ninety." Chase grinned. "I turned twenty-seven a couple weeks ago."

"Did you have a big party?"

"Your grandmother made me a special cupcake, does that count?"

"That's a big no, Chase. Do better next year."

"I'll see what I can do."

Chase prepared the whipped cream while Ruby took a seat at the kitchen island and watched. He kept an eye on her in his periphery, enjoying having her in his space. *I need to get her back here...* He decided he should make her breakfast sometime.

"Where do you land on the breakfast for dinner thing?" Chase asked, scooping the chilled cream into a bowl and carrying it along with plates and forks to where Ruby was sitting.

"I absolutely do not associate with people who don't enjoy breakfast for dinner," Ruby replied quickly. "Do you have a pie server?"

"Oh, yeah." Chase stepped back into the kitchen area and continued. "I'm thinking I need to make you some grits sometime. I wouldn't be doing my southern duty if I didn't."

"Can you even buy grits here?" Ruby asked, watching him cut and serve her an enormous slice of pie.

"We should warm these, shouldn't we?" Chase asked, grabbing their plates and heading toward the microwave. "I've never seen them here, but I imagine you could get them somewhere. I just order them online."

Chase came back to the table with the slices and slid the whipped cream to Ruby. "Bon appétit."

She closed her eyes and inhaled as she brought the fork to her mouth. The aroma followed by the bite filled her senses with memories of fall. "Mmmm... good call on warming it."

"It really is good. How bad would it be if we ate the entire pie right now?"

"We might regret it later, but that's something for future Chase and Ruby to deal with."

"Alright, let's see what we can do," Chase said with a fork salute and a crooked smile. "I think Ms. Millie's apple pie is the best I've had."

"She says her secret is sautéing the apples in butter before putting them in the crust."

"Secret's out now, I guess." Chase grinned.

"You'll have to share your whipped cream secret. It's perfect!"

"Thank you! But there's no secret. I'm pretty sure it's just standard whipped cream. But I'm glad you like it." *You'd like my grits too if you'd come for breakfast.*

"So, how long have you been painting?" Ruby asked between bites.

"I've been interested in art-type things for as long as I can remember. In middle school, though, I had this amazing teacher. She cared so deeply and wanted every child to feel like an artist, but I think she noticed some of my natural talent and took a special interest in me. I had painted before, but she really helped me 'unlock more of my hidden potential,' as she would say."

"Wow. You know, I've recently thought a lot about how we have the ability to affect the lives of the people around us, whether positively or negatively. It makes me want to put more into the interactions I have." Ruby smiled, then took another bite of pie.

"She was the definition of that, I think." *I wonder if Mrs. Simpson is still around.*

They sat in comfortable silence for a minute. Enjoying their pie, lost in their own thoughts. *I think she may be worth it. Worth the risk. She's leaving, but we could figure it out.* Chase saw that her beauty on the outside was more than matched on the inside. *How can I get her here for breakfast without begging? And I wonder what she would say if I asked to paint her. Too soon, probably. Yeah, definitely too soon for that.*

"Why do you work at the spa if you have these amazing paintings?" She paused briefly. "Oh, that's a rude question, never mind. It's not my business." Ruby's cheeks tinted pink and she faced her plate, taking another bite.

"It's fine. I've always hoped it would be possible to sell my paintings and be a full-time professional artist, but I don't think I ever really believed it was possible until recently. I think I have some pieces that are really worth something now."

"The finished one I saw is spectacular. Really breathtaking. You could certainly sell that for a lot." Ruby spoke excitedly, momentarily forgetting about her pie.

In that moment, he decided he would one day give that painting to her. She loved it and eventually it would be hers. *In fact, take all my paintings.*

"That means a lot. I just need to figure out the best way to sell. There isn't a gallery around here. But with the internet, I'm not sure if that's necessary."

"I have no idea, but if you ever want to try the gallery route, there's a beautiful little gallery where I'm from. I'm not sure what they could get versus one in a larger city, but maybe artists start out in smaller galleries anyway?"

"Maybe so. Thanks for the idea, I may very well do that." *Looks like I'll be taking some paintings and heading to Vermont in the fall.*

· · · ● · ● · · ·

They were finishing up their second extra-large slices when Ruby put her elbows on the table and her face in her hands. "Uhhhhhh... I've made a mistaaaaake."

"Me too. I think it would be a waste of time for either of us to enter a pie eating contest." Chase felt fine.

"I don't know if I'll ever be able to eat apple pie again."

"Yeah, I hear that." *I'll probably have another piece after dinner.*

"I should go," Ruby said, standing and carrying her dishes to the kitchen. "Can I put these in the dishwasher for you?"

"No, thanks. Just set them there and I'll get it in a bit."

Ruby seemed to linger, perhaps not wanting to leave but not having a reason to stay. "Okay, well, thanks for sharing your pie with me."

"Well, don't rush off," Chase said in imitation of his gran.

"Wow. That was extremely southern. It was shocking."

"Good thing the southern accent is so charming."

"No, I said shocking, not charming."

"Maybe, but we both know what you were thinking," Chase said, leaning against the kitchen island and giving Ruby his most charming smile.

"Do we?" She raised her eyebrows and smirked. "See ya around, Chase."

She stopped by the door to the porch. "Let me know when I *ken* come *git* me some of them tasty *gre-ets*."

Ruby turned, leaving Chase stunned and momentarily stuck to the island. Eventually he followed her out and called from the door, "That fake accent was extremely offensive!"

Ruby smiled broadly and waved.

That smile is magic. I think I'm addicted.

24

Ruby

HAD CHASE NOT BEEN standing at the door to his house, Ruby would have likely sat in her car a long while, processing all the interactions she and Chase had just had. As things were, she put the car in reverse and backed out of the driveway, not daring to look to where she knew he was still watching.

I just sent out some major flirt vibes teasing him about his accent. That is not what I need to be doing. Nothing had changed, she was still leaving in a few weeks. And she was there to spend time with Mamu and help her, not make friends and be gone. *And I just told him I'd come try grits. I want to. Man, I want to, and maybe if I show up early, he'll be shirtless, chopping wood. I wonder if I could find a big dead tree to throw in his yard the night before... Ruby Butler, you're an idiot. Stop this right now.*

But Chase walking towards her, practically glittering in the sunlight, was playing on repeat in her mind. Ruby couldn't shake it, despite low to moderate effort at doing so. She pulled into her parking space behind the bakery and sat, waiting on her thoughts to stop spinning.

She had practically invited him to visit her in Vermont. *I'd love to see him there, and show him all my favorite things.* "Ugh! Control yourself." Ruby rested her forehead on the steering wheel. "You do not need a boyfriend who lives over five hours away. You couldn't trust him, plus it would just be too hard."

Feeling as if things were settled, she got out of the car and headed straight to Mamu's RV. Without knocking, Ruby opened the door and barged in to find her grandmother cutting vegetables.

"Ruby darling, have I told you lately how grateful I am that you're here?"

Ruby had burst into the RV fully intending to point fingers and accuse her grandmother of meddling in her business, forcing her and Chase together. But there stood her sweet grandmother, the picture of innocence. *Yeah right. Here stands Amelia Butler, the most mischievous grandmother to ever live.* She decided she'd give it some more time before throwing around accusations. She might actually be innocent.

"Hi, Mamu. Whatcha making?"

"I'm prepping my veggies for making some stock tomorrow. Gerald is taking me out tonight, so I don't need to cook. Gotta love that!"

"Where are you going?"

"I don't know. He's being awfully secretive."

"Ooh la la. Sounds like you're in for a fun night." Ruby grinned at her grandmother. "Be home by ten, okay?"

"Yeah, yeah." Mamu rolled her eyes and waved her off. "Did you take the pie to Chase?"

"I just got back."

"I thought you left to go over there a couple hours ago."

"I did. He shared his pie with me, just like you said," Ruby said, reconsidering her decision not to accuse.

"He's a good one, that Chase. How was he doing?"

"He seemed fine."

"Good. Good." Mamu paused, scraping all her veggies into a big bowl. "I heard he's going to be at the dance."

"Good for him. I'm sure he'll have a nice time."

"Oh, I'm sure he will." *Did she mean something by that?* Ruby began to regret not saying anything.

Before she could throw out an accusation, her grandmother spoke. "Well, I need to get in the shower so I'll be ready on time. Did you need something or just stopping by?"

"Just stopping by. Have fun tonight! I can't wait to hear what you do." *We'll talk later, Sneaky.*

· · · ● · ● · · · ·

Up in her apartment, Ruby pulled out all the ingredients she needed to make dinner, only to realize she was still far too full from the pie. *Now what am I going to do?* She needed distractions so she didn't daydream about Chase and all his alluring qualities. *It's a fact that he's kind, fun and gorgeous, but do I need to linger on it? No, I do not.*

Ruby decided to head down to the bakery and make another batch of cookie dough for the dance.

Mamu "heard" he was going to the dance. Ruby would bet she had spies all over town. Maybe she could do her part in the bakery and then skip the dance. She decided she'd give it a shot. *That way, Mamu can't ask Chase to dance, then feign hip pain and call me over to take her place. I'm on to your schemes, Granny.*

· · · · •· • · · · ·

Ruby's phone rang as she was turning on the mixer. She pulled it out of her pocket, seeing that it was her brother.

"Charlie!" She answered, turning off the mixer and sitting in the kitchen's rickety chair.

"Hey, sis. What's happening?" Charlie responded brightly.

"Just baking. Not much else." *Definitely not seeing shirtless near-lumberjacks and acting like a moron, then flirting even though things can go nowhere.*

"That sounds awful—you need to have some fun."

"Baking is fun."

"Doubtful. How's Mamu? I talked to her the other night, and she said she was fine, but you know how she is. She could be laying in a hospital bed for all I know."

Ruby laughed. "Well, this time, I think fine would be accurate. She's still taking it easy, but I think she's recovering well."

"Nice."

"Yeah. Ready for your first day tomorrow, Sergeant?"

"I plan on starting as a captain, thank you very much."

"Oh, my mistake," Ruby said, grinning. She loved her brother, but they rarely spoke since he was not a "phone person." Her being out of town really ate at their connection.

"I'm ready and excited. There's a hot woman in my class."

"Charlie! That's not why you're there."

"I know, I know. But it's an added perk."

Ruby could hear the smile in his voice. "Promise me you're going to focus on what's important and stay safe."

"Yeah, of course. I can't help it if she tries to distract me, though."

"Charlie!"

Charlie laughed. "I promise I'll be focused."

"Good!"

"I gotta run, but I'll talk to ya later, okay? And try to have some fun, yeah?"

"Yeah, yeah. Talk to ya soon. Love you! Miss you!"

"Love ya, ya big nerd."

Charlie hung up before Ruby could respond.

· · · ● · ● · · ·

After making the dough portion of the bakery's most popular item, apple pie cookies, she showered and collapsed in her bed. *This day has been too much. Maybe I should call Vera and tell her about Chase and all the things.*

She was reaching for her phone when a text notification pinged.

Unknown Number: Hey, Ruby, this is Chase. I got your number from Ms. Millie, I hope that's ok.

Ruby's heart rate climbed and she sat up in her bed, not knowing how to feel about this.

Unknown Number: You said to let you know about breakfast for dinner, but I didn't have a way to get in touch with you apart from stopping by.

Ruby saw the typing bubble and waited. *I guess he's going to go ahead and propose a time. Oh, he stopped typing. Maybe he's waiting on me. Did I turn off my read receipts on this new phone?* She checked her settings, and sure enough, he had seen that she had read his messages. Ruby sighed and began typing.

Ruby: Hey. Yeah, that's fine. I do look forward to trying grits sometime.

There, that was good. Friendly, but not too friendly. I really do want to try the grits. I'd be dumb not to when an actual southerner offered to make me some.

Unknown Number: I promise you won't regret it.

Unknown Number: Well, I guess I can't promise you'll like them, but I hope you will.

Ruby: I hope you don't get me hooked on something I don't know how to properly make and can't easily buy in Vermont.

Reminder, I am moving.

Unknown Number: I'm sure I can help you out if you fall in love with them. Which, TBH, is likely.

Ruby: Haha. We'll see.

Unknown Number: I know you were just over here, but I have breakfast for dinner on my meal plan for tomorrow, if you'd like to come.

Ruby: You have a meal plan>

Ruby: ?

Unknown Number: I'm a planner, I can't help it.

I love that.

Ruby: Yeah, I could do that. Sounds good.

Unknown Number: Good. Wanna come around 6?

Ruby: Yeah, I'll be there.

Unknown Number: Good deal. Night, Ruby.

I don't know why, but that feels oddly intimate. How to respond...?

Ruby: See ya tomorrow.

25

Chase

CHASE SET HIS PHONE on his nightstand and stared at his ceiling, a small smile on his face. *She's coming. And I told her I have a meal plan.* He chuckled, turning onto his side. *I bet she has a meal plan too. Maybe one day we'll combine our meal plans.* Chase laughed so hard his bed shook. He was truly happy and hopeful for the first time in a long, long time.

Okay, what should we have with our grits? Eggs, obviously. Sausage. I wonder if she likes sausage? Maybe I should text her and ask. Chase grabbed his phone but placed it back down. No. He didn't want to scare her with too many texts right away. If she didn't like any of the basic breakfast items, she would have said. *I could get Mom's recipe for that french toast casserole, although...*

Tuck and Hershey were suddenly barking like maniacs. Chase got up, pulled on a shirt and headed toward the racket they were making on the screened porch. Both dogs were hyperfocused on one spot toward the backyard. Chase couldn't make out any movement or sounds with his human senses. He flipped on the outdoor lights, but the light apparently didn't reach where the dog-offending whatever was hanging around.

Chase went to the living room and grabbed the fire iron from the hearth, just in case. Then he slipped outside, being careful not to let his barking dogs out with him. Hershey ran over to the door, wanting to go. "Sorry, pal. If it's something dangerous, I don't want you getting yourself hurt."

Chase saw Hershey giving him side-eye as he walked away from the house. "Don't give me that attitude after you got me out of bed."

He continued on, using his phone flashlight, heading toward the dark. When he arrived at the edge of the woods, he shined his light around, not seeing anything until he aimed it lower. There trapped under a massive fallen branch was a huge possum. At least Chase thought it was huge. He had never seen a possum up close.

The possum was hissing at Chase and struggling to get out from under the branch. *I can't believe I didn't hear this branch fall. I guess my mind was otherwise occupied.* The dogs must have heard the possum thrashing about after their attention was drawn by the branch.

"Okay. If I pick up this branch, will you attack me?" Chase stood considering things for a moment. "I'm gonna take your silence as a good sign." *I've got to stop talking to animals so much. I'm not a cartoon princess.*

Chase dropped the fire iron, because there was no way he could lift this branch one-handed. He had his doubts about it with both hands. He set up his phone so the light was shining toward the scene and headed over slowly so as not to spook the animal any more than it was already. He squatted down, wrapping his arms around the branch as far from the possum as he could get. *Man, what an ugly thing.* He stood, lifting the branch and keeping his eyes glued to the possum. Once it realized it was no longer pinned down, the possum scurried away from Chase and into the woods.

"Hasta la vista," Chase said, turning and heading back to his still-barking dogs.

· · · ● · ● · · · ·

Chase was up early for his only massage of the day, after which he took some painting supplies and headed to a trail just outside of town. He set up in a stream of light on a large boulder overlooking a tumbling creek. Chase painted for a while but decided it wasn't what he really wanted to do. He lay down, closing his eyes, enjoying the sound. *Hersh would have loved this place.*

His thoughts didn't go back to Hershey as often as they once had. It had been nearly a decade since Hershey was lost. Memories often hit him for the strangest reasons—the smell of movie theater popcorn, the sight of children sliding down a slide—but this time was no surprise. One of his favorite memories with Hershey was playing together in the creek near his house.

Chase surprised himself when he realized he had been lost in his memories and felt happy. He thought he might know why. *Hersh, I've met an incredible girl.*

· · • · • · • · • · ·

Midafternoon, Chase started the grits because, as any good south-erner knows, you've got to cook grits for a long time at the lowest temperature possible after the initial boil.

He settled onto the sofa and called his mom.

"It's my favorite son!"

"Hey, Mom. Can you tell me how to make that french toast casserole you make at Christmas?"

"I'm doing fine. But your dad is grouchy today—he's cleaning out the gutters. Never did that after last fall. How are you?"

Chase sighed. "Sorry, Mom. I'm good."

"What's the casserole for? Having some people over?"

"Just one person. But I'm into having leftovers."

"Hmmm... would this person have a hearty appetite? Or perhaps a more dainty appetite?"

Stealthy questions, Mom.

"I guess we'll just have to wait and see."

"So, it's a girl. Have you met a girl, Chase?"

Well, this is not why I called.

Chase sighed for the second time in as many minutes. "I have made a friend, who happens to be a girl. She's coming for breakfast for dinner tonight."

"Chase!!!!" He jerked the phone away from his ear. "This is won-derful! Tell me all about her! What's her name?"

Chase told his mom about Ruby, in the shortest amount of words she would let him get away with. She gave him the recipe and he headed back to the kitchen to continue preparing for what he considered to be his first real date in ages, whether Ruby realized it or not.

· · · · ●· · ● · · · ·

At 5:59 Chase heard a timid knocking on his door. He took off practically running to answer. *Okay, take it down a notch. You're going to freak her out.* He paused a moment and then opened the door to be greeted by the most genuinely beautiful smile he had ever seen. It stole his breath for a moment. *She's truly a masterpiece.*

"Welcome to breakfast, madam." *Madam? What's wrong with me?* Chase waved her into his home.

"Thank you, sir. It's a pleasure to be here." Ruby grinned, apparently unfazed by their trip back in time. "It smells amazing in here. Did you make cinnamon rolls?"

"I'm afraid that was not one of the things I learned during my time at the bakery. It's my mom's french toast casserole. I'm pretty heavy-handed with the cinnamon."

"Oooo. I've never had a french toast casserole. This will be a meal of firsts." Ruby smiled, setting down a poppy-covered ceramic bowl. "I brought some fruit. I hope that goes with what you already have going on."

"Fruit always goes. Thanks!" He grabbed the bowl and headed to the kitchen. "I'll put it in the fridge until I get this finished up. We're close, I just need to cook the eggs."

"Cold eggs are the worst, so I appreciate that. Can I do anything?"

"Actually, yeah. I meant to make some coffee but got caught up with other things. Would you mind? It just feels right with breakfast, don't you think? I got some decaf."

"No problem at all. I've been told that I make wonderful coffee. I can't confirm that it's the best in the US, but it probably is."

Play cocky, I love it. Man, I could get used to her being here. "You'll find I'm a very discerning coffee judge, so we'll see," Chase said, looking at her with his best condescending face before turning to the eggs. "Coffee things are in the cabinet above the pot."

"You mind if I put a dash of cinnamon in with the grounds?"

"Oh, definitely do that."

Chase grabbed the cinnamon and turned to Ruby as she was turning to him, effectively pinning her between himself and the counter. He felt his heart rate picking up as he stared down into her deep green eyes and felt the heat coming off her body. *Step back, Chase, she barely likes you. But I want to be closer. So much closer.*

26

Ruby

I CAN'T BREATHE. THE look on his beautiful face is so intense. I want to touch him. Grab his shirt and pull him toward me.

Chase stepped back, smiling and handing Ruby the cinnamon, acting like nothing had happened. She took it from him, nonplussed. *Realistically, he was probably standing there for three seconds, but it felt like ten minutes. What just happened? I don't think we actually even touched, but it felt like he was covering me like a blanket.* His presence was overwhelming. Ruby took a deep breath. *Shake it off, Ruby, and make the coffee.*

She turned from where she had been frozen in thought, staring at Chase's back as he returned to the eggs. *Why does he have the heat on in the summer? I might have to step outside when I get the coffee going.* Ruby grabbed the end of her shirt, pulling it back and forth away from her body for some airflow.

"Are you hot? I'll turn the air up." Chase moved toward the hallway, pulling the eggs off the burner.

"No. I'm fine. Just..." Ruby pushed her glasses up her nose.

"Just?" Chase gave her a lazy grin.

"I was hot for a minute, but I'm fine now." Ruby turned back to the coffeepot, even though she had finished her task. "How do you take your coffee?" she asked, pulling two mugs from the cabinet.

"Usually just some cream. Had I been thinking, I would have made us some whipped cream."

"I think you've done plenty," Ruby said, looking around at the spread he had prepared. He had obviously gone to a lot of trouble for her. *He surely wouldn't have done this if he had just been cooking for himself.*

Chase pulled out plates and forks while Ruby poured them each some coffee and carried the mugs to the table.

"Help yourself," he said, handing her a plate and stepping away from the counter. "I hope you like sausage."

"It's not bacon, but it's good." Ruby grinned widely and Chase's answering laugh and smile made her heart flutter.

"True, true." He grabbed a plate for himself. "We often made breakfast bowls at home with grits on the bottom, eggs, sausage and a sprinkle of cheese on top. So I thought you needed sausage with your first grits."

Ruby looked down at her plate, where she had all her food separate. "I think I've made the opposite of a breakfast bowl."

"Next time."

Next time, huh?

"Or perhaps if I have seconds."

"I'd say *when* you have seconds. You'll want more, I can feel it." Ruby knew chances were high she would want more food. But she also knew she couldn't want more of anything else.

Ruby and Chase took their seats at the kitchen table. She stared at her plate, not sure what to say. Unwilling to do anything to deepen whatever they had going on here. Protecting her heart because she wasn't moving. *I love my school so much and moving is a big deal. I can't get invested in this guy. Plus, Ethan was nice at the beginning. Who's to say Chase won't turn out the same?*

"What are you waiting for? I can't wait to see you dig in."

"No pressure." She rolled her eyes comically. "What if I hate them?"

"You won't."

"You have a lot of confidence in this pile of mush."

"There you go again being offensive," Chase said with mock disappointment, shaking his head.

Ruby smiled. "Okay, okay. I'm digging in."

Chase stared, eagerly awaiting her reaction. *So good.* She couldn't believe she had been missing this her entire life. She took a bite with sausage and eggs. *Oh yes. His family knew what they were doing.*

"Given that you've taken multiple bites and not spoken, I'm guessing you like them? Not that I'm surprised."

"You've changed my life, Chase." Ruby shoveled in another bite. She thought she saw a twinkle in his eyes as he began eating, continuing to watch her enjoy her meal. *Look at that beautiful smile.* Ruby suspected he would change her life too, if she'd let him. She couldn't let that happen.

"Sometimes change is good, huh?" Chase asked with a small smile.

"So it would seem." *And that's what I'm afraid of.*

. . . . ● . ● . . . .

Ruby and Chase ate their meal with minimal chatting, and what chatting happened, Ruby tried to keep surface-level. She was determined not to get to know him better, because she had a feeling she would really like what she learned. *I'm leaving. I don't want to move to Maine, and who would move to Vermont for someone they've known only for weeks?*

"So, are you going to the dance Friday?" Chase asked as he finished his second plate. "Those things are a pretty big deal."

"So I've heard. Yeah, I'll be there manning the bakery's table." *Hint: I will not be dancing, so don't get your hopes up.*

"Good deal, I'll make sure and come get a cookie. Are you making the apple pie ones?"

"Naturally."

"Nice. You'll have to walk around the silent auction. There's always some good stuff. I'll probably be over there most of the time. There's one item I need to monitor."

I wonder what that's about.

"I told my mom I would bring her something fun from Maine, so this might be a good chance. I'd like to get her something that doesn't come from a souvenir shop, ya know?"

"Yeah, I'm sure you can find something there. I hear Mrs. Maxwell has donated some of her blueberry preserves, canned blueberry pie filling and some other blueberry-type products she's made. That could be a fun gift," Chase said with a shrug as he cleared their plates.

Ruby followed him into the kitchen with their mugs.

"Would you like more coffee? We could go sit on the porch—it's probably nice out," Chase asked as she was heading to the sink with the mugs.

That sounded wonderful to Ruby, so cozy. But also too much like a date. *I don't want him to get the wrong idea and feel like this is something it's not.*

"I would, but I have to get up early tomorrow to get some cinnamon rolls going. Mamu's gal pals are having a big brunch for their inaugural book club meeting in the morning. Honestly, though, I'm not sure Mamu knows how to read, so I don't know why she's getting involved with the book club."

Chase smiled, although she thought she saw disappointment flit across his face for a moment. "I'm glad you were able to come tonight. It was fun sharing grits with you. And your coffee was great. Best in the Northeast at least."

"The cinnamon really kicks it up a notch, doesn't it?"

"I'm definitely glad you thought to add the cinnamon."

Ruby could feel her cheeks heating as she remembered their moment with the cinnamon. "Can I help you clean up? I'd like to," Ruby said, changing the subject. She picked up the nearest dish and headed to the sink.

"I'd say no, but I'm pretty sure you're going to insist and I am rather ready to relax, so yes, please. I think we can knock this out pretty quickly."

Ruby and Chase worked in companionable silence and all without another cinnamon-type incident. Much to Ruby's dismay? Relief?

"Thanks for having me for dinner. Everything was so good and I appreciate all the work you put into it."

"You're welcome, Bee. I was glad to have someone to share my grits with."

Bee, again. Why do I love that so much?

27

Chase

As soon as Ruby left, Chase started painting. He felt inspired. He had several colors on the palette in his hand when Tuck ran into the room and jumped up on him, getting paint on Chase's shirt and face.

"Oh, gee thanks, man." Chase pulled off his shirt and took it to the laundry room to soak, cleaned his face in the bathroom and headed back to the screened porch to see what else needed cleaning. The dogs started their manic barking and Chase looked outside and saw Ruby's car headed back toward his house. He looked down at his bare chest. *I probably have time to put on a shirt.* "Nah." He smiled. *I think I'm going to have to use everything I've got to get this girl, plus I really loved seeing her blush last time.* Chase laughed to himself and stepped toward the door.

He waited until he knew she was about to knock and opened the door. "I'm afraid I haven't had a chance to make any more grits, if that's why you're back."

Ruby just stared at him for what he imagined she would categorize as an embarrassingly long amount of time. He watched her wide eyes and the pink coloring her cheeks, then the realization that she had been staring dawned on her face and her eyes locked with his.

Chase couldn't get enough of flustered Ruby. Her beauty was enhanced by the way her rubescent cheeks made the green of her eyes stand out.

"So what brings you back, Bee?"

Ruby shook her head, clearing her thoughts. She locked her eyes on his, obviously purposely not looking anywhere else.

"I left my fruit. I realized when I was halfway back to the bakery that we hadn't gotten it out of the fridge."

"I'm so sorry, that's on me. I guess I shouldn't have stuck it in there to begin with. Come on in." Chase held the door open in such a way that she had to walk under his arm. "I love fruit. It would have been great with our meal."

"So how did you manage to lose your shirt in the little bit of time since I left?"

"There was a dog and paint incident. Somehow I was the only casualty."

Chase walked into the house toward the refrigerator, Ruby trailing behind him. He grabbed the fruit and turned back to her.

"Would you like to keep some?" Ruby asked as he was handing her the bowl. "Have it with breakfast? I probably won't eat it all before it starts to go bad."

"I'd love some, if you're sure. I do hate for things to get wasted."

"Absolutely. Just save me some watermelon—it's my favorite."

Chase stopped midway to the cabinet with his containers, turned and grinned. "It's my favorite too. But I'll save you some." *I'll leave every last piece for you.*

• • • • • • • • • •

The next morning, after a breakfast of steel-cut oats and watermelon-free fruit, Chase got a phone call from an unknown number.

"Chase? This is Denise Maxwell, the coordinator for the fundraiser dances."

"Yes, Mrs. Maxwell, I know who you are." *You're the one who guilted me into saying yes to something I'm very much not looking forward to.*

"Ah, well, you never know, do you? Anyway, I was just calling because the dance is only three days away and we need to know your date plans so we can get the card ready. Are you excited? I bet it will be thrilling to be bid on. Don't you think?"

"I'm not sure, I just hope it raises a lot of money." *Then perhaps it will feel worth it.*

"Oh, honey, we've been hyping it up and the feeling I get is hundreds."

These people cannot be that desperate.

"Oh wow."

"I don't think you realize how highly sought after you are. I was just—"

"Well, I am glad to help," Chase interrupted before she could tell him any more about how many women wanted him. "I plan to take her to a food truck and have a picnic by the lake and then take a canoe out onto the water. Does that sound like a good plan?"

"Sounds lovely, dear. *Oh!* You should plan the canoe ride for sunset. Wouldn't that be lovely? I can't imagine a more magical date."

"I'll see what I can do. I need to run, I've got to get to the spa."

"Okay, dear, you have a great day and we'll see you Friday."

"You too. See ya then."

Chase's phone buzzed as he was headed out the door.

Green-Eyed Ruby: I just finished my fruit and it reminded me how good dinner was last night. Thanks again! :)

She texted me. Which means she thought about me. This is good. Okay, what's the right response...? "I had my fruit too, it was delicious." No. "It was great hanging out. Maybe we should do it again another time?" No. I don't want to ask her out on a date over text. Plus she doesn't even know we're dating in my head. "Come eat grits anytime." Nah. "You're the most fun, smart and beautiful woman I've ever had the pleasure of spending time with. Can I come find you right now and hold you till the afternoon?" That would go over well.

Chase: You're so welcome. I was glad to do it. Thank you for the delicious fruit! I had a great time hanging out! And I feel like I really accomplished something with the grits. Let me know when you start craving them again.

Green-Eyed Ruby: I might be one and done with grits.

Chase: You're not. I saw your face.

Green-Eyed Ruby: Fine. I'll probably be in touch.

Maybe the way to Ruby's heart is through her stomach. Chase smiled to himself and headed toward the spa, hope blossoming in his heart.

28

Ruby

"I never asked you about your date the other night. How was it?"

Ruby and Mamu were putting out some sourdough sub rolls to rise, the finished product heading to Gerald's shop that afternoon.

"It was lovely. He got several bouquets of flowers and set them around the shop. He said he wanted us to have a special date where we met. There were candles and he made Julia Child's beef bourguignon."

"Wow, that sounds amazing. Is he a good cook?"

"He really is. I'm telling you, find a man who can cook."

"I'll keep that in mind." It seemed Chase could really cook. Not that it mattered. The memory of him making that whipped cream like it was no big deal played in her mind. Then there was all he had done last night. *I didn't mention it at the time, but I think those were the best scrambled eggs I've ever had. I wouldn't hate it if he cooked for me more often.*

Ruby was deep in her unwelcome but also very welcome thoughts when she heard the bell on the door jingle. She took off her gloves and headed to the front.

"Ruuuuuuuuuubeeeeeee!" She heard Vera's voice before she saw her. She ran and launched herself at her friend, throwing her arms around her neck. "Surprise! I thought for sure Mamu was going to give it away, but I guess I was wrong."

"I had no idea you'd be here a week early! And Mamu knew? Sneaky."

"Oh, she had me all planned to be here right after you said you were coming. It was my idea to keep it a secret. You know how I love to surprise people."

"And yet, somehow, you hate to be surprised," Ruby said, disentangling herself from her friend.

"I've never claimed to make sense." Vera took a turn around the bakery's storefront. "This place is really great. Several pretty spots for photos. You really should have an Instagram page," she added to Mamu, who was headed in her direction for a big hug.

"I was just telling her that," Ruby said with raised eyebrows at her grandmother.

"Yes, yes," Mamu said, releasing Vera. "And *I* was just telling *Ruby* that I'm not interested in the social medias. If somebody else wants to run a page, fine by me."

"We'll see what we can do," Vera said, putting her arm around Mamu's shoulders. "I get the feeling Ruby will be around a lot."

"Vera, I have a job that isn't here. And while I love Mamu, I have no plans to uproot my life."

"We'll see," Vera said, heading to peruse the cookies in the case.

· · · · ● · ● · · · ·

Vera kept Ruby and Mamu company in the kitchen until it was time for lunch. Ruby took her friend up to her apartment for sandwiches and the cookies Vera had stolen while perusing the shop and kitchen.

"So, when do I get to meet Chase?" Vera asked, putting her ham and cheese on the pan to grill.

"I thought you came to see me."

"I can have multiple purposes. You're the main one, yes, but I feel heavily invested in Chase at this point."

"I don't know why."

"You've told me, in detail, about every interaction you guys have had. At least as far as I know. I'm still upset you didn't get that pic of him lumberjacking."

"I told you I would send you a pic of a lumberjack *if* I saw one. Which I haven't because he is not a lumberjack."

"Semantics." Vera waved her hand dismissively, then flipped her sandwich. It wasn't browned in the least.

"Let me cook your sandwich," Ruby said, stepping toward the stove and taking the spatula from Vera's hand.

"I'm just saying. I'd like to meet him."

"I could get you an appointment for a massage."

"Are you paying?"

Ruby just gave her a look.

"Mamu arranged for someone to help her tomorrow, so you can show me around. Got any ideas for places we can go?"

"Honestly, I haven't seen much myself. Mostly, I've been to the same places just right around here."

"You know who would know the best stuff around here?"

"I'm not asking Chase to show us around."

"I was going to say you should ask him for recommendations, but I like that much better."

What have I done? "We don't need to ask him anything. We'll just look around and find all the awesome spots ourselves."

Vera turned her puppy dog eyes on Ruby. "But don't you want me to have the most amazing visit ever? I'm afraid tour guide Chase is the only way."

"Are you making yourself cry?"

"These are genuine tears shimmering in my eyes."

Ruby rolled her non-shimmering eyes. "I'll text him for recommendations, but I'm not asking him to show us around. He's probably busy anyway." Ruby put more butter in the pan and flipped Vera's sandwich. She turned to her left to see Vera standing, arms crossed, leaning against the counter.

"What's going on, V?"

"Just waiting on you to text Chase before you *forget*."

Ruby stared at Vera for a beat, then turned back to the sandwich. Vera cleared her throat.

"Okay, okay," Ruby said, resigned, handing Vera the spatula. "Give your sandwich another minute. I'll send him a message." Ruby pulled her phone from her pocket.

Ruby: Hey. My friend Vera surprised me and showed up this morning. She wants me to show her around tomorrow. Do you have any "can't miss" suggestions?

"Happy now?" Ruby sat at the table with Vera and stared down at her cold turkey sandwich, wishing it was a toasty warm grilled cheese.

"For now," Vera said, mischief in her eyes.

· · · ● · ● · · ·

Half an hour later, the two Butlers and Vera were in the bakery, rolling snickerdoodle dough balls in a cinnamon-sugar mixture. *Will I ever be able to think of cinnamon normally again? Oh my gosh, I'm getting hot just thinking about him so close, looking down at me with those beautiful blue eyes.* She tried to still her thoughts and took a deep breath, which was heavily laced with cinnamon. *Freakin' cinnamon.*

Ruby's phone buzzed, so she took off her gloves and slid it out of her pocket.

Unknown Number: Hey! Sorry, I was with a client. I have some ideas. It would be easier to just take y'all around, if you'd like. I have a massage at 8, but otherwise, I'm free tomorrow.

He wants to take us around. Of course he does.

29

Chase

CHASE FINISHED WITH HIS only client for the day and got into his dark blue SUV, whistling to himself. *Today is going to be a good day.*

He pulled up to the bakery and before he could get out, Ruby and her dark-haired friend came out the door toward him. Chase hopped out to open their doors. Ruby's friend, Vera, had a wide smile on her face and an obvious pep to her step. Ruby, on the other hand, was dragging her feet and scowling. Well, not scowling, but she certainly didn't look excited. *I'll put a smile on her face before long.* Chase suddenly worried her facial expression had to do with him. *I've inserted myself into their visit.* He hadn't thought about that fact when he'd offered. He didn't want his happiness causing her to be unhappy.

"Hey! Good m—" Chase started as they approached.

"Chase, I'm assuming?" Vera interrupted, squeezing him in a quick hug. "I'm Vera. Great to finally meet you!"

Finally?

"It's nice to meet you too," Chase said, trying to wipe the confusion from his face. "Good morning, Bee." He couldn't help giving her what he assumed was an extremely cheesy smile. He turned in time to see Vera mouthing "Bee" to her friend with raised eyebrows and a smile. Ruby narrowed her eyes at her.

"Good morning. Ready?"

"Well," Chase responded, "I got to thinking, I sort of invited myself into your visit. I know Vera didn't come here to see me. I was thinking I could send—"

"Don't be silly. We want you to join us. I can't think of a better way to spend the day than with my best friend and her new friend." Vera was all giant smiles and hand motions.

"Well, I'm not sure if Ruby considers me a friend or not, but I hope so." He smiled at Ruby and turned back to Vera. "I'll leave it up to you guys. I'd be glad to go, but I'd also be glad to just send you some ideas."

"You're going," Vera said with finality.

"Ruby?" Chase asked.

"You should come. It will probably be better than me just showing her around."

"Okay, if you're sure."

Chase headed around the car, and Vera climbed into the back, leaving the front for Ruby. *As I had hoped.* Chase suppressed a smile. *That seat can always be yours if you want it.*

"So how would you like to go to a shop that sells the most interesting and random things?"

"A perfect first stop," Vera called from the back.

· · · ● · ● · ● · ● · · ·

The trio pulled up to the Treasure Trove as Chase was finishing telling them all he knew about the store. It was owned by a middle-aged woman who went to yard sales every single Saturday, weather permitting. She bought the most unique or rare finds she could unearth and stocked her store with them. Given the size of their town and the relative remoteness of it, she did a lot of driving to neighboring areas. Chase had gotten his mom a beautiful teapot from there for Christmas last year, and he had gotten his dad a vintage Han Solo figurine.

They walked into the store, Chase going one way and the girls going the other. He walked around, not shopping for anything or anyone in particular, but you never knew what might jump out at you at the Treasure Trove. Chase was checking out a life-size cutout of an obscure NASCAR driver when he heard his name.

"Hey, Chase!" Vera called from across the room. "Which purse should Ruby get? She can't decide." Vera held up a hunter-green purse and a big straw bag. He felt quite unqualified to help with this.

"Well, will everything you want to carry around fit in the green one?"

"I think so," Ruby said.

"I guess my vote goes to the green one. It goes with your eyes." Chase turned, walking back toward where he had previously been. He heard Vera whisper, "It goes with your eyes." He looked back over at them and saw Ruby put the green bag back and pick up the straw bag. *Guess it bothered her that I mentioned her eyes. Or maybe she just liked the straw bag better.* Chase had a feeling it was the former. *That's okay, Ruby, that's okay.*

Chase and the girls meandered through the store for almost an hour. When they headed to checkout, Chase had found a handmade wooden frame he wanted to use for one of his smaller paintings. Ruby placed her straw bag, a marble chess set and a miniature blue glass globe on the counter. *I love that globe.*

"Hey, guys, should I get both of these coats?" Vera asked, holding up a trench coat and a creamy-colored wool coat.

"That wool coat is the thing of dreams. I'd get that and leave the trench," Ruby answered, taking her receipt.

Note to self: cream wool coats are dreamy.

· · · ● · ● · ● · · ·

"So I was thinking that next we would get some things for a picnic lunch and take a little hike to the actual Laurel Falls. What do y'all think?" Chase buckled his seat belt and turned toward the girls.

"I guess that's the reason you suggested we wear bathing suits?" Ruby said, raising an eyebrow at him.

"I just assumed he wanted to see your sweet little body in less clothing," Vera said with a smirk.

"Vera!" Ruby whipped around in her seat, making a terrible face at her friend.

While I can't say this didn't occur to me, it wasn't my main motivation. He had really just wanted to show them his favorite place. And he knew they would want to swim.

"That sounds great," Vera said, unfazed by her friend's reprimand. "What are we getting for lunch?"

"Well, it's almost eleven, so Slice It Up will be serving sandwiches soon. But I'm sure you've eaten that a lot, Ruby, so we could do something different. I was just thinking of food that would travel well to the falls."

"You're right, I have eaten there a lot. Something different would be fun. Don't tell Gerald." Ruby smiled, letting out a small laugh.

"I'm sure we could find something at the diner. Their menu is about ten pages long."

· · · · ● · ● · · · ·

The trio ended up getting a variety of foods to share, including fries for the car because, as Vera said, "nobody likes cold fries."

"Alright," Chase said, opening the back of his SUV. "We can put the food in the backpack and pour our waters into these water bottles." Ruby took the fries out of the plastic bag, then loaded up the backpack while Vera and Chase worked on the waters.

"Were you a Boy Scout?" Vera asked before opening the fries and taking the first greasy bites.

"No. Why?"

"Because they say Boy Scouts are always prepared."

"He's just a planner," Ruby interjected, snatching the fries from Vera and heading to her place in the car.

"A planner, eh? Sounds like somebody else I know," Vera said to Chase with raised eyebrows and a nod to Ruby.

Am I reading too much into this and her earlier comments or is she Team Chase and Ruby? That would be ultra-good news.

Chase smiled to himself, cranking up and heading toward the trail. He forgot to get any of the fries.

30

Ruby

THE THREE STOPPED IN awe of the scene before them. Laurel Falls, the actual falls, was like no other place Ruby had ever been. The main waterfall was about forty feet tall. It was flanked on each side by smaller waterfalls. There was an almost perfectly round pool at the bottom. The most beautiful part, however, was all the tiny round pools, almost like stone pots, formed by at least a dozen little waterfalls. Some pots just large enough to step in, others large enough to wade around in. If that weren't enough, the magical water scene was surrounded by the most beautiful greenery Ruby had ever seen. *This place is gorgeous. Like a place inside of a dream, although I don't think my brain is that creative.*

"No wonder they named the town after this place," Ruby whispered, her wide eyes taking everything in.

"Rumor has it the other name considered was Buttsville, for the town's founder, Henri Butts. But surely that isn't true. I have to believe the people back then realized that shouldn't even be an option."

"Laurel Falls does have a better ring to it," Ruby said, taking off her shoes.

"But imagine how well you could market a place named Buttsville," Vera added with a wide smile and a laugh.

Ruby rolled her eyes and laughed at her friend. *I bet this is something she'll bring up often with new ideas.* She walked over to a bush that looked much like a smaller version of rhododendron with unusual and delicate-looking white and pale pink flowers.

"Chase, do you know what type of bush this is?"

"That's mountain laurel. I'm surprised you haven't seen it in Vermont."

"I mean, maybe I forgot. Or maybe I've just never seen it in bloom."

Chase leaned closer, pulling a bloom closer toward their faces. Ruby could feel her heart rate increase as she felt his warmth at her shoulder. "These are my favorite flowers. There just isn't anything like them." He brushed the bloom gently with his free hand, then released it and headed back toward the water. Ruby's thoughts were a jumbled mess, filled with his delicate touch and surrounding presence. *I told myself not to fall for Chase.* She could feel herself leaning toward self-disobedience, knowing it could lead to nothing good.

After she collected herself, Ruby turned back toward the water. Chase and Vera had already shed their outer layers and stepped into the main pool. Shirtless Chase again. *Is he trying to kill me? Come on, Ruby, that should be old news by now.*

"Get in, Ruby! The water's chilly, but not too bad," Vera called, dragging her hands along the surface. He smiled and disappeared into the water. When he resurfaced, he busied himself looking away from where Ruby was removing her shirt and shorts. *Is he purposely letting me undress in privacy? How thoughtful of him. Why is he so nice? Makes it so hard to keep him at a distance.*

"Take it off, Ruby!" Vera yelled, as if Ruby was helicoptering her shirt above her head. *I wonder if my shirt would make an effective gag for her.*

She was wearing her favorite swimsuit, a black two-piece with small white polka dots. The print along with its high waist made it feel retro, which she loved. She made her way quickly into the water until it reached above her knees and she let out a gasp. "You guys seriously misled me about how cold the water is," she chastised.

Ruby turned her eyes toward Chase the moment he turned to her. The look in his eyes was brief, but she didn't miss it, nor did she miss the halting of his breath or the bobbing of his Adam's apple when he swallowed. *I guess I don't have to be so embarrassed by my lumberjack reaction.* She tried to hide her smirk.

Ruby eventually got used to the water and really enjoyed it. They swam and floated, and they visited all the other little pots, which was Ruby's favorite part. She took so many staged and candid photos in that area. "Ohh! Let's sit on the edge of this one and pretend like we're getting a pedicure." She motioned Vera over and handed Chase her phone. "Please," she said, smiling up at him.

"Of course," Chase said indulgently, taking the photo and handing her back the phone. "How adventurous are you guys feeling? Because you see that ledge on the left waterfall? It's safe for people to jump from when the water level is high like this."

"I'm in!" Vera exclaimed at the same time Ruby asked, "How deep is the water?"

"I'm not sure, but I've done it many times and only ever barely touched the bottom. I imagine I would go much further down than either of you, but we could go over there and try to swim to the bottom, if it would make you feel better." Chase stepped out of the pot he was standing in and headed toward the main pool. The girls followed him and after swimming and diving down, they decided it should be okay—but they still wanted him to go first.

He scrambled up the path, offering his hand to Vera, then Ruby, to help them through a more difficult part. Her breath caught at the contact. Her mind had gone back, far too often, to the touches they had shared that night in the truck. While she would never admit it to herself, she had been waiting and longing for more contact with Chase, so when their hands met, it fulfilled a desire within her that she hadn't fully realized was there.

What is it about this guy? Her heart was pounding, but not from what they were about to do. It was actually not as high as it had seemed from below. She felt as if her body was trying to tell her, "This is the guy." But her brain knew the logistics were too difficult and she couldn't deal with Ethan 2.0. Ruby watched Chase jump and could see his face from the side. *Look at the joy on that beautiful face. I'm not sure I could get used to that face even if I saw it for the rest of my life.*

"Ruby, you go next," Vera said in her ear. "Maybe Chase will catch you." She winked and stepped back.

"I'm beginning to think you're a schemer like Mamu."

"Me? Of course not."

Ruby shook her head and jumped without much thought. The thrill of the drop was over quickly. She slipped into the water with very little splash and, enjoying the sense of weightlessness, she floated as slowly as possible to the surface. When she emerged and opened her eyes, she saw Chase frantically swimming toward her. He looked up and toward her, fear, then relief in his eyes.

"I didn't think you were ever going to surface. You shot down into the water so seamlessly, I thought maybe you hadn't slowed down enough and hit the bottom." Chase stopped, having to catch his breath.

"No heroics needed today." Ruby smiled. *Oh my gosh, I would never survive it if he had to save me.*

Chase didn't have a response. He let out a huge breath and turned to move and make room for Vera's jump.

· · · ● · ● · · · ·

After several more jumps, the crew decided it was time to move to their next stop of the day. They enjoyed their picnic while drip-drying on the big rocks on the bank.

"Ready? I'm more than excited for whatever Chase has for us next, if it's anything as good as the first two stops," Vera said, pulling her shirt over her head.

"This will be hard to beat or even come close to really," Ruby said, gathering their trash.

"The question is, was this better than grits?" Chase asked with a wide smile.

"It's a close call!" Ruby laughed, feeling more carefree than she had in a long time.

Ruby, Vera and Chase were about halfway down the trail when Ruby's foot became trapped in a root and she fell. "Ahhhhhh! Oh, oh, oh!"

"Ruby!" Chase and Vera yelled in unison.

Ruby wiped at tears and sighed, still on the ground. *Why is it always me that junk like this always happens to?*

Vera gave her a hand up and she tried to stand but was not able. "Ahhhh!" She reached out, grabbing for anything she could get a hold of, and found an arm of each of her companions. "Let me hold on to you and see if I can walk." Ruby took a deep breath and cautiously stepped forward. "No. No. No. Nope. That's not happening." *Could I not just watch where I'm walking and be safe for once in my life?*

"I can carry you piggyback, if Vera will take the bag," Chase said, handing Vera the bag.

"Oh, that's okay. I'll be fine in a minute."

"Don't be silly, Ruby. You need him to give you a ride." Vera smirked.

Here she is showing her full Mamu colors. Ruby sighed again. Who was she kidding? She wasn't going to be walking out of there on that throbbing ankle.

"Alright, let's do it, I guess."

Chase stepped in front of Ruby and squatted down. She put her arms around his neck and he locked his arms under her thighs.

"Ready? That feel okay?"

No, I'm beyond embarrassed and can't stand how good it feels to be up against your back.

"I guess so. Thank you."

"Not a problem in the least."

"My dad jokingly calls me Ruby Grace."

"I didn't see your fall, but I imagine it was extremely graceful." Chase grinned over his shoulder. "What's your real middle name?"

"Carolyn, after my other grandmother."

"Believe it or not, my mom used to have a cat named Carolyn," Chase said with a chuckle, adjusting her higher on his back. Ruby laughed, letting go of some of the tension she was carrying.

Vera kept lingering back, to be even with Ruby, giving her smiles that said, "Look at you on Chase's back, he should be your boyfriend." Finally, Ruby mouthed, "Stop that right now."

They continued on for a few minutes when Ruby caught Vera studying her ankle. Vera looked up at her. "It's really swelling dangling like this. I think he might have to come up with a different way to carry you where your foot can be elevated."

You little schemer. He is not going to be carrying me bridal style. But Ruby looked down toward her injury and knew Vera was right.

Chase, who had stopped walking, squatted down for Ruby to get off his back. "I'm pretty sure I can make it with you in my arms if you can keep your injured leg pointing upward."

Ruby sighed, because what else was she going to do? Vera wasn't making the least bit of effort to hide her smile.

Chase turned and put one arm behind her back and used the other to pick her up behind the knees. She held on to his neck to try to help out. *Oh my gosh—and I thought hanging on his back felt nice. Too bad he put his shirt back on. Ruby!* She just needed to get back to the bakery, ice her ankle and get some distance.

31

Chase

AND JUST WHEN CHASE thought the day couldn't get better for him personally, here he was holding her in his arms. Obviously he would much rather she had not gotten hurt. But with the situation as it was, he was enjoying the feel of her in his arms. Probably too much. *She feels so right here. I want her to be mine. I think I'm beginning to be hers.*

Ruby let out a frustrated sigh and rested her head on her arm and against his neck. *Her hair smells so nice. Almost like an orange creamsicle, plus the creek water.*

"I feel like such an idiot. I'm always the one stuff like this happens to. You'd think I was a reckless person."

"You're obviously not an idiot. These things happen. Just last week, I was carrying some empty boxes down the porch steps at home and fell. Thankfully, I wasn't hurt, but it has to be the dumbest thing I've done in a while and I'm sure it looked ridiculous."

"Hate I missed that," Ruby laughed.

That's better.

"I'm sure you do. I'm betting you'd be the type of person who would bring it back up often if you *had* seen it."

"Oh, I absolutely would." Ruby lifted her head and grinned at him. "Not if you had been injured, but since you weren't, I definitely would."

Chase saw the trailhead in the distance and slowed ever so slightly. He was not ready to let her go. He remembered going to church with his friend Tyrell in seventh or eighth grade. The pastor was talking about husbands loving their wives. He said, "My wife is the cheese in my macaroni." *I want Ruby to be my cheese.*

· · · · ●· ●· · · ·

After breakfast the next morning, Chase decided his next painting would be of Laurel Falls. He was sitting on his sofa doing a quick sketch when a thought dawned on him. *Ruby might not be able to go to the dance tonight.*

> **Chase:** Hey, Bee. How are you? How's the ankle?
> **Green-eyed Ruby:** Blech. Mamu is treating me like
> a child.
> **Chase:** Are you able to walk?
> **Green-eyed Ruby:** If hobbling counts.
> **Chase:** I guess it does.
> **Chase:** Are you helping with the cookie baking?

Green-eyed Ruby: Of course not. I told M there were certainly things I could do, but she told me to rest. She has Gerald and Kelsey down there working.

Hmmm... how should I ask about the dance without coming off as too eager? Before he could formulate a new text, she messaged again.

Green-eyed Ruby: She still wants me to go to the dance, but I'd have to stay glued to a chair, which is fine by me anyway.
Chase: Sounds like a good plan.

Is it too soon for me to tell her I'll hold her up so we can dance? Yeah. It's probably too soon.

Chase: Maybe you'll dance next time.

With me.

Green-eyed Ruby: Haha. I doubt it. Who would I dance with?

Is that a little bit of flirting? Me. You would dance with me.

Green-eyed Ruby: JK the pain meds are getting to me, plus I think I'll be gone before the next dance.

So this is my only dancing chance? I really would love to hold her and dance. We'll see what happens.

Chase: What meds are you on?

Green-eyed Ruby: Ibuprofen

Chase: That explains it.

Chase: *GIF of Michael Scott saying "Absolutely, but not really"*

Green-eyed Ruby: Haha. I think I'm going to attempt a nap. I'll see ya tonight.

Chase: Rest well.

Chase: Save me a dance?

Green-eyed Ruby: Real funny. Bye, Chase.

Chase: *Peace sign emoji*

· · • · • · • · · ·

Chase walked up to the large wooden barn wearing dark jeans and a charcoal button-up with the sleeves rolled up. He moved slowly, taking everything in. There was greenery draped around the entrance, the massive doors propped open by huge potted purple hydrangeas.

When he stepped inside, he was surprised by how nice everything looked. He hadn't had high expectations for a barn dance. There were twinkling lights netted across the ceiling. High tables, each with a small arrangement of white hydrangeas, lined the left and right walls. Chase headed toward the back wall, where there seemed to be auction items, drinks and—the real draw—cookies.

As he walked, "Amazed" by Lonestar began to play. He stopped in his tracks when he spotted Ruby sitting behind the cookie table. She had curled her hair and pinned it up. Her lips were tinted dark pink. *She is so beautiful I think I may short-circuit. If I get any closer to her, she'll probably be able to hear my heart over the music. I want to hold her, sway with her, kiss her...*

Chase calmed himself as best he could and continued. Before she noticed Chase, he saw what she was doing. She was singing to the music. He laughed as he approached. "I thought you didn't like country."

"I didn't say I had *never* liked country."

"I'll give you that. You seemed pretty into what you were just singing."

"I did like it, way back when. I was just singing because I like to sing and I remember the words."

"So why did you give up on country?" Chase asked while looking at the many cookie options.

"There are too many sad songs," she said, chin on her fist as she looked up at Chase. "And songs about cheating. I don't want to hear those either."

"That's fair. I hope none you personally relate to, though."

"Unfortunately, I've felt a little like Carrie Underwood in 'Before He Cheats' before."

"No. He must have been the biggest idiot on the planet." *What moron would let her slip away, much less cheat on her? How dare he. Maybe I can figure out who he is…*

She gave a little chuckle and shrugged. "I like to think so."

"You look gorgeous, by the way." Chase gave her a half smile, when really he wanted to grin widely, take her in his arms and show her just how gorgeous he thought she was.

"Thanks, you clean up pretty well yourself." She grinned.

Her smile is going to kill me.

"I did shower and make extra effort with my hair."

Ruby laughed. "It shows."

Chase noticed a line starting to form behind him. "I'll get out of the way, but I'll see ya later."

Ruby gave him a small wave and he headed toward the auction table, acting like he was looking for something to bid on, but really he just wanted to see what was happening on his paper. Toward the middle, right between a card for "Dog Grooming" and one for "A Sweatshirt with Personalization," was "The Date of a Lifetime with Chase Davidson." *Mrs. Maxwell!!* Chase was horrified. The dance had just started, so there were no names bidding on the date yet. *I ought to just stick this paper in my pocket and slip away.*

"Hey, pal! Whatcha bidding on?" Vera came to stand beside Chase, and much to his chagrin, her eyes went immediately to the "date of a lifetime."

"This was not my doing," he said with a frustrated growl before Vera could comment.

Vera looked at him with something he couldn't place sparkling in her big brown eyes. "Well, this is interesting. It just so happens that I love to canoe."

And just like that, Chase's item had its first bid.

. . . • . • • . . .

Vera rushed to the dance floor when "YMCA" began to play. As Chase watched her go, he saw Ainsley walking through the barn doors. *Nope. Nope. Nope.* Chase took off back toward Ruby and the cookie table.

"Can I hide here? I saw someone who will definitely ask me to dance, and I'm really not interested in dancing with her. I'll put a chair back in the shadows."

"I mean, you're welcome to try to hide here in the imaginary shadows. You can use Mamu's chair—she's dancing. Or actually, Gerald is holding her up and swaying them around the dance floor."

Does that give you any ideas? We could do that. "That's nice, looks like they're having fun dancing like that," Chase said after spotting them on the dance floor. He wondered if he should just ask her, or if that would mess up the friendship they were building.

"I saw your date donation. Someone thinks highly of himself," Ruby said, raising her eyebrows at Chase.

Of course she saw it.

"I got roped into that and I certainly had nothing to do with the wording. I already told the woman who runs this that I won't be doing it again."

"Oh, you might have spoken too soon. Who knows, the future Mrs.... you know what? I don't know your last name."

"It's Davidson."

"Okay. So the future Mrs. Davidson could be in this very room during the next dance. And it all could start with the very date you got roped into."

Not for the next dance since you won't be here, but I suppose it's possible for today's dance. You should go bid.

"Are you going to bid?" *Well, that just slipped out.*

"I'm sure I'll bid on something," Ruby replied with a crooked grin. "That quilt is stunning. I also might need that cutting board shaped like Maine. And like I said, I need to get something for my mom."

"A lot of nice options, for sure."

They sat watching the dance and selling cookies. Chase hoped Ainsley (or any of the other girls) didn't decide she needed a cookie.

"It's really beautiful in here, isn't it?" Ruby asked, eyes traveling around the room.

"It is. It's much better than I expected."

"Same. I'd forgotten you haven't been before. What made you decide to come this time?"

It was you, you absolute beauty.

"I just figured it was time."

· · · • · • · • · ·

Chase's hiding spot proved to be entirely ineffective. Before long, a brunette who looked to be in her early twenties abandoned the cookie line and asked Chase to dance. *I'm too polite for my own good.* Once he was on the dance floor, it was over for him. He spent much of the remainder of the evening with women who either A) talked the entire time about themselves *or* B) let their hands rove much too freely *and* C) weren't Ruby.

He was removing the latest assailant's hands from his butt and stepping away from her when Vera joined him on the dance floor. "Just outbid somebody named Ainsley for the canoe fun," Vera said, stepping in to dance with Chase. "Also, Ruby seems to be feeling up for a dance."

Chase followed Vera's indicated direction and sure enough, there was Ruby, being held and supported by another man, swaying with him to the beat of a romantic country song. Chase was frozen for only a moment before he started making his way across the room, leaving Vera smirking behind him.

32

Ruby

Ruby couldn't quite identify the feeling she had while watching Chase dance with woman after woman. She liked to think it wasn't jealousy, but she knew deep down it was. In fact, she was shocked by how strong the feeling had hit her. Ruby didn't like feeling like this, so when a nice-looking man approached the table and asked her to dance, she said yes without much thought. It was only when they were walking out to the dance floor that she remembered her ankle. She explained what was going on and that she would have to lean heavily on him. He seemed a little overeager about holding her up while dancing. The dance itself was really rather awkward and Ruby was counting the seconds until the song would reach its end. She considered calling it quits mid-song, but she didn't. She wanted Chase to see her dancing with someone else, not that she would ever admit that, even to herself.

As the song was ending, Ruby spotted Chase heading her way. *The look on his face is so intensely focused. I love it.* He looked down at her ankle, concern coloring his features. He reached them quicker than she thought possible.

"Hey, man, I got it from here," Chase said, offering Ruby his arm. She took it, glad to release her hold on the other guy.

"Oh, okay. Thanks for the dance," he added awkwardly to Ruby before turning and heading toward the drink table.

"Are you okay?" Chase asked, adjusting to support her better as they headed back toward the cookie table.

"No. I guess I got jealous." *Oh, I've got to fix that.* "Of all the dancing. I love to dance, so when he asked, I threw caution to the wind. Clearly that was a mistake."

Chase helped her onto her chair. "Do you need ice or anything? The dance seems to be wrapping up. I can help you to your car."

"I rode with Mamu, plus I need to help her get this stuff packed up."

"Nonsense," Mamu interjected. "Get a ride with Chase. Gerald is here to help..."

"And me too," Vera added helpfully.

"That settles it," Chase said. "The auction just ended—I'm going to go pick up my cards. Rest a minute and I'll be back to help you out."

When he was gone, Ruby turned to Vera and her grandmother. "You two sure seem eager to get rid of me. Why is that? Huh?"

Twin looks of innocence covered their faces. "We would never want to be rid of you," Mamu said, standing and folding her chair.

"We just know what's best for you right now is getting a ride back with Chase and getting that foot elevated."

"Yeah, listen to us," Vera added. "We know what's best for you." Mamu play-slapped Vera's arm.

Chase returned, looking relieved. "Vera, you won the date! I'm so glad it's you and that this is over. I know you aren't here much longer, so how about tomorrow?"

"Sure thing."

"I'll pick you up at six, if that works."

"Perfect. See you then!"

• • • • • • • • • •

"What's the best way for me to help you out of here? I'm assuming you don't want me to carry you, but I'd be glad to."

Did his face just look hopeful? In truth, Ruby would love nothing more than for him to carry her out, but she also wanted to hold on to what dignity and distance she could.

"How about I put my arm over your shoulders and lean on you?"

"I'm not sure our height difference is really conducive to that sort of help, but we can give it a shot."

They did, and Ruby was sure it was the most awkward thing anyone had ever done. Once they were outside, she looked around and found the parking area empty of people.

"This is ridiculous—please carry me to the car."

"I thought you'd never ask." He bent and swept her up before she could blink. "This is so much easier."

Ruby laid her head against his shoulder. She felt ridiculous, enjoying this as much as she did. It was simply a thirty-second walk to his car. *Oh, who am I kidding?* She loved feeling his muscles move and his arms supporting her. *Maybe I'll ask him to forget the SUV altogether and just carry me back to the bakery.*

Before she knew it, he was setting her down and opening her door. Once they were both inside, she opened her purse and pulled out a cookie. "I saved this for you," Ruby said, handing the cookie to Chase. "It's an apple pie cookie. I thought you might enjoy it, since apple pie is your favorite dessert."

He looked touched when he smiled, accepting the cookie.

Don't read too much into this, Chase. It's just a cookie.

"When Ms. Millie gave me my first one, it was the best cookie I had ever had. It's still my favorite. Thanks so much." His entire face smiled before unwrapping the cookie and backing out of the parking spot.

Once inside the bakery, Chase carried Ruby to a chair near the counter. "Park here a sec. I'll be right back."

He wasn't gone very long, and when he came back he was carrying a bag of ice. "Alright, onward and upward."

Okay, once again, I have got to get some distance back in this relationship. Friendship. I can't have him carrying me over the threshold of my apartment. Can't have him getting ideas.

"I think it would be easier for me to try to walk up the stairs. It's a narrow staircase and I think I can lean on the rail and be okay."

"Whatever you think. I'll walk behind you in case you need assistance."

It was a slow and arduous journey up the stairs. *I can do this. People do difficult things all the time. This is nothing. I think I might be sore tomorrow from all this awkward...*

"Ahhhhh! Excuse you?!"

Chase had grabbed Ruby around the middle and continued walking up the stairs like nothing had changed.

"That looked terrible and I couldn't take it anymore," he said, taking the last few steps with ease.

Ruby opened the door to her apartment and he continued forward and helped her onto the sofa.

"Where can I find a towel to wrap the ice?"

"In the drawer to the left of the stove."

If it wouldn't be weird, I would ask him to carry me everywhere. Ugh. Distance. Distance. She was still leaving before long and had no desire to move.

Chase returned from the kitchen and situated the ice on Ruby's elevated ankle.

"To be honest," he said, "I'm not sure ice is appropriate now, but I assume it won't hurt."

Ruby opened her mouth to speak but was stopped by the loudest stomach growl she had ever heard. It sounded like he had a literal bear trapped behind those beautiful abs.

"I'm no expert, but it seems you might be hungry."

"Well, I didn't have dinner. I wrongly assumed there would be dinner-type food tonight. I think my body was okay until that cookie reminded my stomach that it needed sustenance."

"I have salad stuff I didn't finish. Veggies and grilled chicken in the fridge. Nuts and croutons in the pantry."

"You don't have to feed me."

"I insist." *Because apparently I can't let him leave.* "You've done a lot for me the past couple days. Plus I owe you a meal and this is the easy way out."

"I've never felt like you owed me a meal. But if that were the case, would leftovers count?"

"I'm pretty sure, but I could check the rule book."

"No need. I've got the rule book memorized and it says the original intent of the food has to be to serve it to the other for it to count as debt satisfaction."

"Is that right?"

"I'm afraid so. So if you feel like you're in my debt, I guess according to the rule book, you still are."

"In that case, I'll pay you back in September."

"You'll be gone in September."

Ruby grinned widely, raising her eyebrows and shrugging. "Precisely."

"We'll see what happens," Chase shot back, heading toward the kitchen and relief for his hungry stomach.

· · · ● · ● · · · ·

SATURDAY 1:00 PM

"I am so tired." —Vera

SATURDAY 3:00 PM

"My body feels weak." —Vera

SATURDAY 5:00 PM

"I've got a headache. Ruby, you might have to take the date," Vera said, rolling over on the couch, where she had spent the majority of the afternoon.

"I'm sure you could reschedule it."

"No, that's rude."

"It is," Mamu chimed in, walking toward Vera with a glass of water. "Let's get you hydrated, dear."

"Thank you. Plus," Vera continued, "when I'm feeling better, I want to spend the rest of my time here with you, not on a rescheduled date." Vera looked at her friend with a sweet smile.

"I'm not going on the date, you schemers. You think I don't see what you're doing, but I'm on to you."

"Oh, don't be silly," Mamu said, patting Ruby's arm. "Vera needs to rest, so you might as well go have fun on the date."

"You two are the schemingest schemers."

"Go get ready, dear. Wear that pretty pink lip gloss you just got."

"No." She decided she was going to wear it, but only because she loved it. That was the only reason. Right?

33

CHASE PULLED UP TO the bakery just before six. He was met at the door by a still-hobbling but surprisingly mobile Ruby. "Hey, Bee. How's your ankle?"

"Somewhat recovered, despite what I thought was going to be a setback last night. Somebody put some ice on it for me. That must have been it."

Chase smiled, in spite of the twinge of sadness he felt as he realized he wouldn't need to carry her anymore. "Whatever it was, I'm so glad to see you on the mend. Is Vera ready?"

"I'm afraid you're stuck with me. Vera isn't feeling well." At his look of concern, she sarcastically added, "Don't worry, I'm sure she'll be completely recovered by morning, if not sooner."

Ruby's face and tone were something Chase couldn't interpret. He wondered if Vera was faking for some reason. He hoped so, because if not, here he was again benefiting from someone else's misfortune. He couldn't believe things had worked out how he'd hoped but had never dreamed they would.

"I hope so. She's only here a couple more days, right?"

"Yeah, she'll be fine," Ruby said, her lack of concern incredibly clear.

Chase sort of enjoyed little-bit-cranky Ruby. *Still, maybe I can turn things around for her. I hope so.*

"Ready, milady?" Chase offered his arm. She threaded her arm through his, grabbing his bicep. He wasn't sure if she was doing this because she wanted his help walking or because they were on a date. *Either way I'll take it!*

· · · · · · · · · ·

"Wait here." Chase hopped out of the SUV and jogged around to open Ruby's door and help her out. He threaded their arms once again and led them towards a food truck called Do the Q. As they got closer, she noticed it was covered in landmark stickers.

"I was thinking the stickers were places they've taken their food truck, but I feel fairly certain these people haven't been serving barbeque at the Eiffel Tower," Ruby said, stopping with Chase at the back of the line.

"I mean, you never know, this is a top-of-the-line food truck. I wouldn't take my date to anything less." *I'd take you anywhere you want to go.*

Chase pulled her ever so slightly closer and they stepped forward in the line and turned so they could see the menu. "Oh!" Ruby hugged and pulled his arm excitedly. "I want the North Carolina

BBQ! It just feels right." She gave him a smile like he had never seen from her. *Did my heart just flutter? Or explode? I love her. I love her? Do I?* Chase was stunned.

He had to recover a moment before he spoke. "I wouldn't do that. Their North Carolina BBQ is a lie and an insult to every North Carolinian."

"Wow. That feels really dramatic. But maybe I would like it since I don't know what it should taste like?"

"I don't think even then it would be good. In North Carolina, depending on where you are, the barbeque is either tomato-and-vinegar-based or pepper-and-vinegar-based. These people seem to have mixed the two types to create the monstrosity they serve."

"I thought this was a top-of-the-line food truck?"

Chase gave Ruby a half smile. "Everything else is delicious."

"I still want it."

"You'll be begging for my brisket."

"Shouldn't I have something from North Carolina today?"

You can have me every day. "I'd say no, but I have a feeling it wouldn't matter." Chase decided he might as well order the large serving of brisket.

Ruby smiled that smile again. Chase was done for.

He took a deep breath to refocus on what he was supposed to be doing. "Alrighty, then. Hush puppies? Fries? Slaw?"

"Yes. All that."

"Ten-four."

· · · • • • • • · ·

The lake was just a five-minute drive down the road and, thankfully, the spot Chase had in mind was free. He asked Ruby to wait in the car while he took the food, drinks and blanket to the plush grass overlooking the lake. He spread the blanket and placed everything on top. When he turned, he wasn't surprised to see Ruby hobbling toward him. "Ruby!" he yelled in semi-sincere reprimand. He ran toward her and she laughed.

"I'm really okay, but thank you." Chase had a hold of her and was trying unsuccessfully to think of valid reasons to pick her up and just carry her to the blanket.

"The ground is uneven."

"It's really fine."

"Well, you never know."

He helped her get settled on the blanket and they took a moment to enjoy the view before getting into their food.

"I love it when trees reflect on water like that," Ruby said, a soft smile on her face.

"A beautiful view," Chase said, looking at Ruby. *That was so corny. I love it.*

Ruby turned, catching his gaze. "Ready to eat?" she asked, reaching for a box.

"I'm ready, but I'm not sure you are." Chase laughed, opening boxes and handing the fake North Carolina BBQ to Ruby. She grinned, opening her fork and digging in. He watched her face go from excitement to grimace as she struggled to chew and swallow her first bite.

She loaded another bite onto her fork and began bringing it toward her mouth. She sighed and dropped the fork. "This is absolutely disgusting. I was going to hold on to my pride and force myself to eat it, but it's just not worth it."

"I'm glad you didn't. I got extra brisket for you."

"Even after I refused to listen?"

"Sometimes you have to make mistakes so you can learn." Chase gave her a look of feigned superiority.

"Lesson learned."

Chase put her barbeque back into the bag and got out a clean plate, which he filled with a generous serving of brisket.

"Not even an 'I told you so'?" Ruby asked, accepting the plate with a smile.

"You've suffered enough."

Ruby took a big bite and moaned, thanking him through a mouthful of brisket.

· · ● · ● · ● · · ·

"I've been whitewater rafting and kayaking, but I've never been in a canoe."

"Wow, is this going to be too tame for you?"

Ruby laughed as Chase dragged the canoe into the water. "No. No. I haven't done anything scary. Only moderate stuff at the most. I just find it funny that I've done those things and never something as simple as canoeing."

Ruby took Chase's hand and he helped lower her into the canoe. She smiled her thanks and turned to look at a ring-necked duck floating not twenty feet away. Chase climbed in, grabbed the oars and pushed them off the shore, sending the duck soaring.

"Did you see the duck flying over the water? That was majestic. I wish I had a photo." Ruby leaned back, hands on the sides of the canoe.

"I bet there are photos of scenes like that all over the internet."

Ruby looked at Chase with an incredulous smile. "But it wouldn't be the one that *we* saw."

Chase smiled back at her, rowing them farther into the water. The silence between them was comfortable as they took in the scenery, enjoying the breeze and the sounds of nature thriving around them. Movement drew their attention as they passed a cove to their right.

"Top of the mornin' to ya!" a man wearing a cherry-red bathrobe, cowboy boots and cream-colored fedora called to them. He was smoking a pipe and standing on the shore on top of a clearly home-made raft, which basically consisted of what appeared to be freshly chopped trees, judging by the leaves still attached in places.

They smiled at the man and Ruby gave him a small wave.

"Come back in an hour, I'm having a party on my yacht! It's black-tie optional!" the man called.

Chase was picking up speed away from the cove. He called back, "Maybe next time, thanks!"

He and Ruby stared at each other wide-eyed until they were far enough that the man wouldn't hear them. Once they passed that invisible barrier, they burst out laughing.

"Top of the mornin' to ya, Ruby!"

"And to you! I'll see ya on the yacht!"

They dissolved into laughter once again. "It's after eight at night!" Ruby exclaimed between hysterical laughs. "Does he have his days and nights mixed up?!"

"He's got something mixed up!"

· · · • · • • · · ·

Chase had rowed them back toward where they'd put in and let the boat drift. It was sunset, and the colors were nearly overwhelming in their subtle beauty. They sat watching the hues change and the clouds shift, the peace of their surroundings enveloping them.

Chase turned to Ruby when she sighed. She kept her eyes to the skies. "Half my time here is already over. It'll be hard to leave. I'm having a really great time here. Vermont is beautiful too, but for whatever reason, I don't have many moments like this. Plus, I'll miss Mamu. And if you keep this up, I'll end up missing you too."

"I'd be honored to be missed by you." *Although, I'd rather you not even have the chance to miss me.*

Ruby turned to him then. They looked into each other's eyes for a couple moments, until Ruby said, "We'll see what happens," and turned back to the sunset.

What does that mean? We'll see if she misses me? We'll see what might happen with us? What will happen at the end of the summer? That was definitely a moment we shared. I want to tell her how I feel, but I don't want to scare her.

Chase reached over, grabbed her hand and gave it a soft squeeze. "We'll see," he said, releasing her and then picking up the oars to guide them back to shore.

34

Ruby

THAT NIGHT, AS RUBY was trying to sleep, she had so many moments from their date on repeat in her mind. She had felt things shift in the boat. *We'll see what happens. We'll see what happens?* What did she mean? What did she want it to mean? Chase liked her and she knew it. He might not think he was obvious about it, but he was. We'll see, he'd said. *I can't let him get his hopes up. Or should I?*

Ruby turned to her side and grabbed her phone. Vera was beside her in a deep sleep. She had fallen asleep instantly, like she hadn't been lounging on the sofa much of the day feigning illness. She hoped to distract herself by scrolling around so she could hopefully fall asleep before the sun started to rise. Distraction, however, would have to wait. Much to her (mostly unacknowledged) delight, she had a few texts waiting on her.

Unknown Number: Hey, Bee. I had a great time tonight. I'm sorry Vera was sick, but I'm not sorry you took her place.

Unknown Number: It's probably obvious, but I'll miss you when you leave.

Unknown Number: See ya at the yacht party.

Chase. What am I going to do? I think I like him. I can't trust him. Freaking Ethan, still ruining things. I can still be friendly, though.

Ruby: Top of the mornin' to ya.

Ruby: Since it's 12:15 in the morning. I can't sleep. Ugh.

Ruby: I had a great time too. Glad I got to go. Don't worry about Vera, she's absolutely fine.

Chase: I'm up too. My brain won't shut up.

Oh! He's up! Why am I so excited to be late-night chatting with him? Calm down, Ruby. The goal was to go to sleep.

Chase: I keep wondering if that man is on his yacht thinking he's entertaining people. And should we have gone??

Chase: *GIF of little girl at a stuffed animal tea party*

Ruby: *Laughing face emoji* That's perfect! And no. We made the right call staying away!

Ruby: What are you up to tomorrow?

Chase: I have appointments starting at nine. I should finish up around four. Why?

Why? I don't know. Here I am, not trying to get him more attached, but apparently I can't help myself. Ugh. I don't like this conflicted feeling.

Ruby: Oh I don't know. Vera and I are helping Mamu with some wedding shower treats tomorrow.
Chase: Good times. Well, let me know if y'all wanna do anything. I'll be around.
Chase: I'm gonna give sleep another shot. Good night, Bee. *Bee emoji*
Ruby: Good luck.
Ruby: Night, Chase. *Smiling emoji*

Oh no.

• • • • ● • ● • • •

The next morning, Ruby and Vera were in the bakery helping Mamu. Her grandmother and friend, of course, wanted to hear all about the date. Ruby told them about the food truck and her ordering mistake. They absolutely cackled when she told them about the man on the raft. Vera slid a pan of heart-shaped sugar cookies into the oven. "You guys should have joined him for his party. Imagine the stories you would have to tell then!"

"If we lived to tell them," Ruby replied, stirring together the filling for some dark chocolate truffles. "I think we made the right choice."

"We'll never know," Vera said with a shrug.

"Mamu, what are you up to tonight? Want to join us for dinner?" *Then we'll have plans and I won't be tempted to message Chase.*

"Another date with Gerald. We're going to where we had our first date. Isn't that sweet?"

"It is! Where was your first date?" Ruby asked.

"We went over to Ellenville and ate at this little Italian place. I had gnocchi with pancetta in cream sauce. It was so good, I could faint just thinking about it. I tried to recreate it once and it did not go well in the least."

"That sounds amazing. Maybe we need to come with you," Vera joked.

"Consider yourselves not invited," Mamu shot back with a smile.

"Wow. That was a dagger to the heart." Vera clutched her chest.

Ruby sighed. "Have fun tonight. That sounds really amazing."

Vera and I will just have to come up with other super-fun plans. Maybe I could find a good gnocchi recipe to try at home. Now I'm craving it.

· · · • · • · · ·

"So what's Chase up to today?" Vera asked, cleaning up her lunch plate in Ruby's apartment.

"Working till four."

Vera smirked. "Know his schedule, do ya?"

"I do not. It just so happens that I know about today. Wipe that smug look off your face, Vera Ann Stephens. I'm going to send you back to Vermont."

"I've got an idea for today." Vera collapsed onto the sofa, ignoring Ruby's threats.

"Oh yeah? Do tell," Ruby said with a raised eyebrow.

"We're going to pull a prank on Chase."

"Pass. Obviously we're too old for that."

"It's just fun, and you're never too old for fun."

"The definition of fun changes as you age."

"I'm not sure that's true."

"Vera, we are not pranking Chase. We are not fifteen-year-olds trying to get a boy's attention."

"Speak for yourself."

· · · ● · ● · · · ·

Since Ruby was nearly powerless against the whims of Vera, she found herself standing outside of Chase's house around 3:20 that afternoon. *Oh my gosh. Am I a fifteen-year-old trying to get his attention? Probably, although I'm pretty sure I already have his attention if I want it. Why do I listen to Vera so easily? I need friends who have less tendency toward illegal activities.*

"Once again, we cannot break into his house."

"It's not breaking in if the window is open."

"I'm not sure that's accurate."

"The point is moot anyway. He wants you in his house, trust me."

"I do not."

Ruby followed Vera through the window at the back of the house into the hallway. *Why do I listen to her?*

"He's going to freak but then love it!" Vera's confidence that he would ultimately love it was what ended up swaying Ruby to agree. Tuck and Hershey, of course, met them at the window. There was barking at first, but once Ruby greeted them, they settled, lying on the hallway rug. The girls continued down the hall and Vera gasped.

"What? What?" Ruby whisper-yelled.

"This painting is gorgeous. I assume it's his? If so, you seriously undersold his talent. This is incredible."

"Yes, it's his."

"Wow." Vera moved on. "This is a cute place, Ruby. Your blanket basket would go perfectly in the corner by the couch."

"Oh my gosh. Stop. Let's get this over with and get out of here."

"Let's do this thing!" Vera whisper-yelled, then smacked Ruby on her rear.

Ruby yelped in surprise. "What the heck, V?!"

"People on teams do that. We're on Team Surprise Chase right now."

Ruby shook her head and continued down the hall.

Their plan, a.k.a. Vera's plan, was to unscrew his showerhead and put a bouillon cube in it, tape down the sprayer at his kitchen sink so it sprayed when he turned on the water and put confetti on top of his kitchen fan blades. *I still can't believe I'm going along with Vera and her teenage ways, but I guess it's too late to turn back now.*

"I'll take care of the kitchen while you do the bathroom," Vera said, handing Ruby a bouillon cube and creeping away from her like a ninja, despite there being nobody in the house.

I'll get Vera if anything goes wrong with this.

$$35$$

Chase

Chase's last client called and rescheduled, so he left the spa shortly after three. He stopped by the store to grab a couple lemons for the chicken dish he was making for dinner, then headed home. He wished Ruby would text—he would text her, but he didn't want to be pushy. He felt like things were going well and didn't want to scare her off.

When he stepped into his house, he thought he heard the dogs into something, but they were lounging on the living room rug. *I guess I imagined that.*

He unloaded his groceries, which of course ended up being more than lemons, then headed to his room to change into some running clothes. He pulled off his dirty pants, shirt and socks and pulled his closet door open. *Someone's in my closet!* Chase reared back and punched. *It's Ruby?!?!* He was able to slow his punch but not stop it completely. Ruby ended up toppling over into his dirty clothes basket.

"Ahhhhh!" Ruby screamed.

"Ruby!" Chase looked at her, panicked. He reached down his hand and helped her up. "I'm so sorry. Are you okay?"

"I see your underwear!"

"Oh!" He bent and grabbed his pants, which had dropped in the chaos. He may or may not have taken longer than was strictly necessary to put them back on. And he may or may not have flexed anything he reasonably could as he did so. He saw her watching from the corner of his eye and smiled to himself. He looked her way before he finished and was pleased to see her face as red as a tomato.

Now to figure out why on earth she's in my closet.

"So... what's new?" Chase asked, crossing his arms and leaning against the wall, a smirk on his face.

Ruby sighed, head in hands, and seemed to take a moment to overcome her embarrassment. She met his eye again, determined to act like the events that had transpired over the past two minutes were no big deal.

"Vera convinced me that we should prank you. She's in the house somewhere. I was in your bathroom when I heard you get home. You're early, by the way." She raised her eyebrows at him. "I escaped the bathroom but heard you coming, so I ducked in here like a teenage burglar and decided I'd hide in the closet until I could make a clear escape. Obviously things didn't quite work out like I'd hoped and here we are."

"So what did you do in my bathroom?"

"Wouldn't you like to know?"

Getting brave again, I see.

"I could press charges. You broke into my house and then tried to creep on me while I was only wearing my underwear."

"First, it's not breaking in if the window is unlocked. Second, I didn't creep on you. If anything, you brought about that situation."

"Okay, *first*, I'm pretty sure that's not true. *Second*, it is absolutely not my fault that you were hiding in my closet, hoping to catch a glimpse."

"Why on earth would I want to catch a glimpse?" Ruby stepped closer to intimidate.

Chase stepped so close you couldn't have slipped a piece of paper between them. "You tell me." He had never wanted to grab someone so badly. Hold her, kiss her and never let her go. Chase was feeling a strange mixture of adrenaline from the home invasion and desire, and all he could do with it was stare down at her as she stared up at him with those moss-green eyes. He was reaching for her when they were figuratively doused with ice-cold water, causing them to jump apart.

"Oh! Well, this is where you guys are." Vera laughed awkwardly. "Should have stayed hidden, I see. Hi, Chase. Good to see you again."

"*Surprised* to see you again. In my house."

"We just couldn't stay away, I guess." Vera shrugged and gave her version of a sheepish grin.

"Y'all wanna stay for dinner? I was fixin' to take a run before, but I'm already hungry, so I could go ahead and get it going. We could eat shortly after five."

"Yes!" Vera shouted at the same time Ruby said, "No, we won't be doing that."

"And why not? We don't have plans, do we?"

"Hang on. Chase just said 'fixin' to' and we need to talk about that," Vera said with a grin.

Ruby ignored her friend. "I wanted to try to make that gnocchi. Plus, is sharing a post-invasion meal typical behavior of burglars and their would-be victims?"

"Of course it is. But technically we aren't burglars since we didn't steal anything. What if we try to make the gnocchi tomorrow night, just the two of us? A going-away dinner."

Ruby sighed and looked at Chase. "Are you sure? This takes inviting yourself over to a whole new level."

She is so precious.

"Absolutely. Come on. Or actually, head on to the kitchen. I'm going to try again to get changed." Chase smiled and headed back to his closet.

· · · • · • · • · · ·

When Chase came into the kitchen, his eyes went straight to Ruby. Her head was hung and she looked defeated. "What's going on, Bee?"

"I'm so embarrassed. I don't typically do asinine things."

Chase took her face in his hands and gently turned her face up toward him. "I'm *so glad* you're here. Whatever prank I'll have to suffer in the bathroom will probably be worth it. No part of me is upset about this or thinks any less of you. So don't think another thing about it." *In fact, this may be in the top ten best things to ever happen to me. Maybe top five.*

Ruby sighed. He released her face and enveloped her in a hug, grateful Vera was making herself scarce. Ruby stood there stiffly for only a moment before she relaxed into him and wrapped her arms around his waist.

"I'm sorry we—"

"Ruby."

"Okay. I won't mention it again."

With extreme reluctance, he released her. "Dinner." He clapped his hands and headed toward the fridge. "When I get this in the oven, there won't be anything to do except wait, so I was thinking we could play cards. What do you think?"

"Yes, let's do that," Vera called from the screened-in porch, where apparently she had been looking at paintings and pretending not to listen to everything that was going on.

Ruby rolled her eyes. "That sounds good to me. I need to use the restroom, but when I come back I can help you with whatever you need."

I need you. "Sounds good."

As soon as Ruby left, Vera showed back up in the kitchen. "As you know, I'm leaving super soon. I just wanted to tell you not to mess this up when I'm gone."

"What?"

"As soon as Mamu told me about you, I knew you could be the one to bring Ruby back to us. Since her very-long-time boyfriend cheated on her in our last year of college, she has trusted nobody. We tried and tried to tell her that not all guys are like that, but she had a lot of resistance to that. She hasn't even dated since. But anyway, I feel good about you, Chase. I've tried to do what I can while I've been here, but you'll still have Mamu while I'm gone."

"This is quite the team event. I didn't realize."

"Ruby deserves to have a team behind her. Even when she doesn't know it."

"So this is why you're here tonight having played a prank. I can't say I don't appreciate it, although I'm not going to get injured, am I?"

"I'm a schemer, not a sadist."

"Good to know."

As Ruby was walking back into the room, Chase opened the chicken and put it in a bowl. He flipped on the faucet to wash his hands and got sprayed right in the chest. He switched it off quickly and continued on as if nothing had happened. The girls dissolved into laughter.

36

Ruby

Sunday night had brought with it lots of laughter and fun over cards and Chase's delicious lemon chicken and veggies. It has also brought into the light a lot of feelings Ruby didn't know what to do with. Instead of letting herself linger on them too long, she threw herself into everything else going on.

Monday night's gnocchi goodbye party was such a special time with just Vera. It reminded Ruby of their good times in college, which made the actual goodbye on Tuesday afternoon simultaneously easier and more difficult.

Wednesday rolled around and Mamu had Ruby in the bakery kitchen, making apple pies for the Independence Day rush. "I learned my first year here that everyone wants an apple pie on the Fourth, but apparently nobody wants to make one," Mamu said, cutting a crust to make the lattice for a pie top. "We have fifteen orders and I thought we would make five extra to take to the parade."

"Tell me more about the parade. Your answer last night of 'it's different' has just piqued my curiosity."

"I'm sorry, I was in a rush last night. The parade is a reverse parade of sorts. All the children who live in the area, active military and veterans walk or ride in the parade. People and businesses cheer and clap and hand out treats to the children. It's a short parade, but it's a lot of fun. Pretty much everyone comes."

"What a fun tradition. I bet the kids love that."

"They seem to. The toddlers are my favorite. They ride with a parent on Mr. Roberts's trailer. I can't wait to see them with their chubby cheeks, waving their little flags, their parents trying not to get poked in the eye."

Ruby laughed. "Well, I'm excited too."

· · · · ● · ● · · · ·

Mamu and Ruby were stepping out the bakery's front door when Ruby felt her phone vibrating in her pocket. She smiled. "A message from Charlie!"

"Tell him I said hi," Mamu said, looking around for Gerald.

> **Charlie:** When u coming back? I wanna book us at that new escape room obstacle course place. It's booking up quick.
> **Ruby:** Mamu says hi.
> **Charlie:** Tell her I said, whats crackin, Mamu?
> **Ruby:** *Eyeroll Emoji*

Ruby: I think I'll be back on the 28th. I'm not sure I want to go there, though. Mom said somebody broke their arm last week.

Charlie: It'll be fine, I'm booking it. Wanna invite Vera?

Ruby: She still isn't interested, Charlie.

Charlie: I know. I've moved on from my childhood crush. Remember the girl from police academy? *big grin emoji* I want to invite her.

Ruby: Is that wise?

Charlie: Does it matter? What if I don't take a chance and miss out? I'd have to be mad at you forever and I don't wanna have to do that.

Ruby: Ugh, alright. I'll ask Vera and let you know.

Charlie: Dope. Catch ya later.

Ruby: SMH. Bye, Charlie.

· · · · ● · ● · · · ·

The parade was, as Ruby suspected, so sweet and special. She was so thankful to have been in Laurel Falls to experience it. The best part, however, was when Mamu pointed out the truck of toddlers heading their way. Out of the corner of her eye, she noticed the driver was not an old man, like she had expected Mr. Roberts to be. It was Chase and her heart exploded at the sight of him.

"Chase!" Ruby and Mamu called from their spot in front of the bakery. He turned and gave them the most beautiful and genuine smile she had ever seen. *My heart can't take this. He's too much.* Ruby was stunned at her sudden wave of feelings. She was hit by how wonderful he truly was. So kind and genuine. She wished their circumstances were different.

"Hey, guys!" Chase called, slowing the truck to nearly a stop.

"What are you doing driving the toddlers?" Mamu asked. Ruby wasn't ready to speak again, content to stare at him in shock at her own feelings.

"Mr. Roberts is my neighbor. His wife walked over this morning and said he had woken not feeling well and asked if I would take over. I usually enjoy just watching the parade, but those babies are so cute, so I said I'd do it." Chase grinned, looking toward Ruby, who simply grinned back, in a shell-shocked sort of way.

"Who could say no to those fat faces?" Mamu said with a look at Ruby. "Alright, you better move on. But we'll see you soon, Chase. Come get some pie sometime."

Chase waved and took off at four miles per hour with his adorable cargo.

"Are there fireworks tonight?" Ruby asked when she was finally able to speak.

"The town doesn't do any, but there's a wealthy couple on the east side of town who does an elaborate show every year. They live on Lake Worsham, so pretty much the whole town shows up and lines the lake where they can. It's gorgeous."

· · • · • · · ·

Ruby: Hey. Long time no see.

Ruby: Well, except for at the parade. Obviously.
Haha.

Ruby: Anyway... are you going to watch the fireworks tonight?

Ruby put down her phone, making herself not stare at the screen until three dots and a new text appeared. *What am I doing? If he was interested, wouldn't he have asked me to see the fireworks with him? Unless he's waiting on me to make a move.* Ruby took a drink of her water and then gave in. Her hand was heading toward her phone when it buzzed.

Chase: I want to, but I don't have any specific plans.
You?

Ruby: I'm going with Mamu and Gerald. I thought
if you didn't have plans you could join us?

Chase: I'd love that! Thanks for the invite.

Ruby: Good! You wanna come to the bakery around
8:30? Gerald says he knows the best spot.

Chase: Sounds good. I look forward to seeing you.

Ruby: *Fireworks emoji*

· · · · • • · · · ·

The fireworks started and just like Mamu said, it was gorgeous. The colors reflecting on the water and the booming echoes off the nearby mountains were a loving assault on the senses.

Movement drew her attention to her left. Gerald was getting down on one knee. Ruby started, grabbed Chase's forearm and bounced up and down. He put his arm around her as they turned to watch and listen. Ruby, so engrossed in what was happening, didn't really register his arm or his proximity.

"Since you came into my life, everything has been lighter, happier and definitely more fun. You are a joy and a beauty. And your kind and generous soul inspires me. I can think of no better way to spend the rest of my days than with you. Millie, will you do me the great honor of becoming my wife?"

Mamu had single tears trailing down from each eye. She smiled and hugged him so aggressively they almost ended up sprawled in the sand. Ruby couldn't hear her grandmother's answer, but she knew it was a yes.

Ruby looked up at Chase with raised eyebrows and a smile. His face was so close. Then she realized his arm was around her. It felt so good and so right. *I want this, but... but what?* Her breathing was coming fast as he just stared down at her. She didn't know what to say or do with the war going on inside her. Chase angled himself toward her and was leaning down. Ruby was opening her mouth to blurt something about not wanting to move when Chase opened his mouth and spoke instead.

"You're a lot like your grandmother, you know." He squeezed her shoulders and released her, turning back to the fireworks. Only a moment passed before he was leaning toward her again, tucking a tendril of hair behind her ear. "And just so you know, it's taking all the restraint in my body to keep from kissing you right now, but this isn't our moment." He ran the backs of his fingers slowly along her jaw, the look in his eyes making it clear that he meant what he said.

Ruby just stared at him as he once again turned back to the fireworks. She could only pay attention to the fireworks inside her.

37

Chase: Thanks again for inviting me to join you guys for the fireworks tonight. I had a blast. (haha) (Does blast work as a pun with fireworks?)

Chase: Anyway, I'm glad I got to be there for Millie and Gerald's engagement.

Green-eyed Ruby: SMH. You're a nerd!

Green-eyed Ruby: I still can't believe they got engaged.

Green-eyed Ruby: He had taken her on a series of special dates, which obviously culminated in this. Pretty romantic.

Chase: Nerd and proud.

Chase: I didn't know Gerald was such a romantic.

Chase: Come have dinner tomorrow.

Green-eyed Ruby: I can't. Mamu is taking me to dinner in Ellenville.

Chase: Come over after?

Green-eyed Ruby: Sure. Eight?

Chase: I'll be here.

Green-eyed Ruby: See ya then. Goodnight, Chase.

Chase: *GIF of a kitten snuggling into bed* Night, Bee.

· · · ● · ● · · · ·

CHASE WAS FEEDING TUCK and Hershey when there was a knock at the side door. *She's early.* Did that mean she was eager to see him? He had hoped to leave her wanting after the fireworks the night before. Perhaps he had.

Chase headed toward the door and saw Ruby through the window. She was looking out toward the woods, the setting sun shining down on her making her seem to glow. *What an angel.*

He opened the door, a crooked smile on his face. "I have something for you."

"Hello to you too." Ruby bent and greeted the enthusiastic dogs as she made her way onto the screened porch. "And hello to you and you."

When Ruby was upright again, Chase engulfed her in a hug. "Hello and welcome." He held her a second longer than a friendship hug and it was not nearly enough.

"Is *that* what you had for me?"

"Dozens of those and also this." He led her across the room and picked up a small painting.

Ruby gasped. "It's from the date. The duck flying. The reflections. Is that a fedora poking out from behind that tree? Chase, I can't believe you painted this. It's beyond amazing."

"I painted it for you. For you to remember your time here and maybe me as well."

"This is really for me? To keep?" Ruby clutched the painting gingerly against her chest. She turned to Chase, eyes wide.

"Yes. That's yours. You can have any of them you'd like, but I did specifically paint that one for you."

"Chase." Her voice was little more than a whisper. She set the painting back on the table and threw her arms around his neck. "I can't believe you did that for me. I love it so, so much."

Chase savored the feeling of his arms around her waist and he knew she was it for him. He drew her closer and said, "I'm so glad you love it."

"I do. But I wouldn't need it to remember you." She loosened her grip on his neck and he released her. "Thank you. Really. I'll put it somewhere really important." She smiled, looking around at the painting setup. "I wish I could paint something for you. I don't know what it would be... maybe a moose hitting a truck?" Laughter burst from them both, bringing much-needed levity.

"We could paint together. Tonight even, if you're up for it. I can't promise a painting of a moose hitting a truck, but we could go for it and see what happens." *In more ways than one.*

"I would love that, but I don't want to get paint on my clothes. And trust me, I would."

"I have a drawer full of painting clothes. You could look through them and see if any would fit well enough."

Ruby took only a moment to consider. "Okay, yeah. Let's do it." *That's awfully forward of you, ma'am.*

• • • • • • • • • •

Ruby walked back onto the screened porch wearing some of Chase's old black running shorts and a shirt he had gotten when he and his family went to Yellowstone when he was seventeen. *She is unbelievably cute.* He loved seeing her in his clothes.

"I've prepared your canvas for you and put some paint on the palate. Do you have any ideas of what you might want to paint? A moose hitting a truck might be a bit much for our first try."

Ruby laughed. "Okay, yeah, that does sound a bit ambitious. I haven't had any ideas. I thought we would just start and see where things go."

"Okay. Maybe start by mixing some colors. It might inspire you."

Chase watched her mix her colors. He showed her the different brush types and the corresponding brushstrokes they could make. He held her hand as she held the brush, showing her the movement of hand and wrist. *Her hand is so soft. And it feels so delicate but still strong.* He wanted to hold that hand, grab her and pull her to him.

He was standing behind her, careful not to crowd too much into her space despite his desire to do so. Chase was still afraid of spooking her and was careful to keep their pace smooth.

He released her hand to let her try the stroke. She made a valiant effort, then turned and looked up at him with those beautiful green eyes. "How was that?"

"Pretty good. One of the great things about painting is that you can generally paint over mistakes or areas you just don't like."

"If I start doing that, my painting will end up being three inches thick."

"I'd like to see a three-inch-thick painting." Chase laughed and went to stand to the side. "Had any inspiration yet?"

"Can we just try to paint a moose? No, because you would have to do basically everything. Ummm..." Ruby touched her chin, thinking, and got white paint on herself. "What about a sunset over a lake? Kinda like what we saw from the canoe."

"That's a great idea, and you've already got some perfect colors mixed up."

Chase was so happy to be creating with her. They worked together for nearly three hours, taking coffee breaks and story breaks. When he pointed out the white paint on her chin, she gave him a spot to match. He had never been happier to have paint on himself. The final product wasn't anything a gallery would want, but Chase loved it.

"This is yours, Chase. I expect it to be displayed in a prominent location." Ruby gave Chase her silliest grin yet as they stood before the easel.

"It will be the most valuable artwork to ever be mine."

· · • • · • · · · ·

It was quite late by the time they decided to call it a night. Chase followed Ruby out to the porch. "Thanks so much for the painting lesson and especially the painting. It means so much to me."

He smiled down at her. "I was so glad to do all of it, Ruby. Thank *you* for coming tonight. Now I have a painting of my own, so we're even."

Ruby laughed and pushed her glasses up her nose. "I'm not sure I'd say we're even."

"I love it and that's what matters."

"And we had fun."

"Truthfully"—Chase ran his fingers through his hair, making it a little wilder than usual—"I haven't enjoyed myself like this in a long time."

Ruby gave him a small smile. "I feel the same way." She hugged him tightly around the middle. Chase sighed internally. *I wish she wasn't leaving. Every time I hold her it's harder to let her go.*

He was startled out of his thoughts by her releasing him and heading to her car.

"Bye, Chase," Ruby called as she was opening the car door.

Before he could respond, his legs were rushing him forward. Ruby turned from where she was putting her things in the back seat. Chase took her face in his hands, his hold gentle but firm. His lips were an inch from hers. "Is this okay?" he breathed, knowing it might break him if she said no.

He felt her nod.

They came together like a tender explosion. Ruby moved her hands up to his chest while he slid his hands back and into her hair.

Even better than I imagined. And he had certainly imagined it. He pulled back to move his hands behind her back, but Ruby was faster. Her hands left his chest and grabbed his shirt at his sides and pulled him to her until they were up against her car. Chase smiled and chuckled against her lips before resuming their kiss.

Chase cupped his hands around the sides of her head. He dragged them slowly down her neck and across to her upper arms, where he pulled her more tightly to him, heart pounding his chest. *She is perfect.* Ruby was clinging to Chase like he was the edge of the cliff and she was hanging on for dear life. He pressed her more firmly against the car and she moaned. He pulled back to look at her, catch his breath and calm the heck down. The rightness of this was all-consuming.

They stared unmoving until Ruby looked down and said, "Chase..." He could tell by her tone that she was about to say something about moving and how it could never work.

"Not tonight, Ruby. Just not tonight." He kissed her gently then, taking his time just in case. She melted into him as he slid his arms behind her back. *I don't think I'll ever be the same.*

When they broke apart for the final time, he took in her beautiful face in the moonlight, then rested his forehead on hers. "Goodnight, Ruby," he whispered, then he kissed her forehead and headed toward his house.

His feelings for her had come on like a tornado. So unexpected and strong, and faster than he would have thought possible. Not even four weeks and everything had changed. *I would do anything, change anything for her.* The realization hit him like a ton of bricks.

He glanced out the porch window and Ruby was still there, frozen against the side of her car.

38

Ruby

Breathe, Ruby. That was by far the best kiss she had ever had. Quite possibly the best moment she had ever had. What made it so good? Was it just that it was Chase? She needed to calm down so she could drive, but her heart seemed to think she'd just sprinted with Olympians. *This is bad. I'm leaving in two weeks. Why did I let this happen?*

"Ahh!" Ruby's phone made her jump.

Chase: Do you need me to drive you home?

Oh my gosh, he knows I'm still out here. Be cool, Ruby.

Ruby: You had to text me to ask instead of just stepping outside?

Chase: I can't be near you again tonight unless you want the sun rising around us the next time we're able to breathe normally.

Oh my. Ruby started doing the opposite of calming down. *Come outside, Chase. No, don't. That's a terrible idea. But it sure wouldn't be terrible at the time. Wait, is he watching me? Oh, I hope not.* She looked at all the windows on that side of the house and didn't see him.

Ruby: And somehow you were going to drive me home?
Chase: I didn't say when.

nkvldnioengnbivdcmeognion

Ruby: Goodnight, Chase.
Chase: Sleep tight, Bee. *Bee emoji*

Somehow, Ruby made it back to her apartment, where she didn't get to sleep until well after two.

. . . .

The next morning, Ruby was awakened by her grandmother sitting on her bed. She was startled, to say the least.

"Late night?" Mamu said with a slightly smug smile.

"Chase gave me a painting lesson."

"Must have been quite the painting lesson. It was after one when I heard your car pull in. Are you a professional artist now?"

"Yes, because one extended art lesson is all it takes. I'll have a painting in the Louvre next month." Ruby got up and headed to the bathroom.

"Chase must be a really good teacher, then."

Are all grandmothers like this?

"I'm not talking to you while I'm using the bathroom," Ruby called as she shut the door. *I think I'll go ahead and do all my bathroom things so if she wants to wait, it will be a while.*

"I'll just go make a pot of coffee."

Ruby sighed. *I'm too tired to deal with her and her "my plan worked" attitude. And yeah, we kissed, but was that her scheme? Or was her scheme for us to date? In my eyes we're just having fun right now until I leave. If I had no other reason not to date him, I might just be spiteful enough not to date him to ruin her plans. But I do have reasons, and they're good ones.*

When she finished in the bathroom, Ruby walked into the kitchen to find her grandmother pouring two cups of coffee. "Do you want cream?" Mamu asked.

"Yes, please. And sugar."

"I think you've probably had enough sugar."

"Mamu!"

"I'm just saying, he kissed you and I can tell."

Ruby took her cup from her grandmother and headed to the apartment door. "I'm going to enjoy my coffee elsewhere."

She let the door slam on Mamu's giddy laughter.

· · · ● · ● · · · ·

Ruby decided she should just get it over with and text Vera about the kiss. She needed to process it a little with someone who might not be as smug as Mamu.

Ruby: You'll be very pleased with yourself when I tell you my news...

Ruby went to click her phone off, but before she could, she saw Vera was already typing. *Shouldn't you be working, Vera? I'm ready to chat, but not really.*

Vera: YOU KISSED MR HOT LUMBERJACK DIDNT YOU?!

Ruby: Yes.

Vera: Buttery Toast! YES!!

Vera: That better not be all that I get.

Ruby: It was amazing ok. Are you happy?

Vera: Obviously I'm happy! I saw a good thing that you were avoiding and worked my magic to push you to make the jump. Why don't I know every detail already? Spill the freaking tea, Ruby!

Ruby: Ugh, ok ok. I was leaving, like getting in my car, and the next thing I knew he had my face in his hands. I don't think I've ever seen anyone smolder, but I think maybe he was smoldering? But anyway, the kiss was so good I absolutely would have fallen down if he hadn't been holding me up.

Vera: Oh heavens—I bet Chase really does have a good smolder. Well, Ruby, what's next? When can I start planning your wedding?

Ruby: Don't get ahead of yourself. I'm still moving back home.

Vera: Ugh, you're a stubborn mule, you know? If it's me that's holding you back—I'll pack up right now.

Ruby: V, obviously you're part of it, but there are so many factors. Find a new man for me back home. New project time.

Ruby: Honestly, it will take me a while to get over Chase. So maybe don't hop on that project just yet.

Vera: I am 100% not abandoning THIS project. I still have time to make you realize you two are the perfect match. We all know Ethan ruined your ability to trust men—we just have to prove to you that you can trust Chase. He's a good one, Ruby.

Ruby: You sound like Mamu. I think she thinks he walks on water. It's possible that I could trust him, but then to also be ok with all the things that would be involved in dating someone in Maine? That's a lot.

Vera: Maybe he does *smolder face* Anyway—I'm proud of you for having the kiss of a lifetime and will continue to encourage you to keep following your heart and stop listening so much to your overly controlling pessimistic mind. Love you—mean it!

Ruby: How dare you.

Ruby: Love you, mean it. *blue heart*

Ruby: Oh, do you want to go to the new escape room obstacle course place when I get back?

Vera: Heck yes, I do. Question is... Are you leaving Maine?

Ruby: I'll be there.

Ruby switched over to her chat with her brother. *Am I leaving Maine? Yes. I think so. Chase is such a complication.*

Ruby: Vera's in to go to that place.

Charlie: Awesome, sis. Can't wait to see you.

· · · · ●·●· · · ·

Later that day, Ruby was by herself, cutting out floral-shaped sugar cookies for an upcoming bridal shower. She was thrilled to be alone to have some space to sort through his feelings. *If I know I'm leaving and not interested in a long-distance relationship or moving, is it leading him on to continue to spend time with him? I think he knows how I feel and he still kissed me.* But she could see it. She could see more with him. A future filled with love and fun. It was pulling her heart apart and she didn't know what to do. *Maybe I need a pro/con list.*

The bakery bell rang and when she cleared the kitchen door, she saw Chase, looking as handsome as ever, wearing his work attire.

Jeez Louise. Can you hear me thinking about you?

"Hey, Bee. I was between clients and I thought I would come get a cookie," Chase said, appearing to seriously consider his cookie choices.

"I just put those white chocolate macadamia nut ones in there."

"Sold."

"So, you came just to buy a cookie?" Ruby asked, putting his cookie onto a napkin and handing it to him.

"Of course not." Chase smiled a smile that made Ruby want to climb over the counter and into his arms. "I wanted to see if you wanted to come eat tacos tonight."

Ruby sighed. Of course she wanted to go eat tacos with him. But was that fair to him? *It might be time to talk about what he asked me not to talk about last night.*

"Chase, I have the best time with you and I really would love to come, but I don't want you to start thinking this is going somewhere it most likely isn't. You know I'm leaving before long. I don't want to see you long-distance and I don't want to move. Like I said, I really would love to come, but more so I don't want to jerk your heart around."

Chase considered that for a moment, his face unreadable. "I want you to come. I'll take what I can while you're here and deal with what comes later, later."

"Are you sure?"

"Without a doubt."

"Okay. What time should I show up?"

"Seven thirty okay? My last massage is a late one."

"I'll be there." Ruby smiled with genuine happiness. She couldn't help it with Chase. He did things to her heart she didn't understand.

39

CHASE HAD QUITE A bit of time before his next massage. He decided to use the time to prepare for taco night with Ruby. He wanted it to be special, to make good use of the time they had left.

When he left the bakery, he went to the grocery store to get a start on dinner. He was rounding the end of an aisle when he ran into Mrs. Maxwell.

"Chase! Oh, I'm so glad I ran into you. I'm already starting preparations for this month's dance and I would really love it if you would offer another date for auction. It was our highest-earning item last time. It would be such a shame for our next cause not to get as much money."

"Hi, Mrs. Maxwell." *I wonder what the next cause is. I'd better not ask, or she will definitely think I'm interested.* "I'm sorry, I'm not going to be doing that again. I would be glad to do another massage, though."

"Oh, no! I do hope you will reconsider, Chase. Think of all the good you could do with that beautiful face of yours, not to mention—"

Chase interrupted her as she started to look down his body. "I'm sorry, but I will not be changing my mind."

Mrs. Maxwell sighed. "Alright, if I can't convince you, then we'll make up for it in other ways."

"I'm sorry to disappoint."

"Okay, dear. You let me know if you have a change of heart. I'm gonna finish up my shopping. I'll see you later on."

"Okay. Bye, Mrs. Maxwell."

What are the chances she asks me every month until I'm in a serious relationship or move? One hundred percent. Absolutely one hundred percent.

Chase checked out and took his groceries home. After he started dinner, he went out and chopped wood for his wood pile. He remembered with fondness the day Ruby had shown up and clearly lusted after him and his sweaty body. He smiled. *I should call her and tell her there's an emergency and she needs to get over here ASAP.*

Instead he snapped what was, he was pretty sure, his very first selfie. *That's not too bad. Suggests what's there. Creates interest.* Chase laughed.

> **Chase:** *Photo* Out chopping wood. I know you like
> it when I do that, so I snapped this pic for you.
> **Green-eyed Ruby:** I don't.
> **Green-eyed Ruby:** I prefer you in coats and multiple

pairs of sweatpants.

Green-eyed Ruby: And a ski mask.

Chase: So you like for me to be dressed as a warm home invader?

Chase: How come you weren't wearing a ski mask when you broke into my house?

Green-eyed Ruby: I thought we weren't bringing that up again?

Chase: It's one of my best memories. Sorry. I even enjoyed the shower that smelled like soup.

Green-eyed Ruby: No, you didn't!

Chase: Ok. No, that was NOT the best *laughing face emoji* But it did make me think of you, which is never a bad thing.

Chase: I gotta get back to it. Go ahead and save that and use it as my contact photo.

Green-eyed Ruby: *photo* Here's one for you.

Chase looked at the photo of Ruby, cross-eyed with a very aggressive growling face. It was a perfect contact photo. *It would be hilarious if I painted this on a huge canvas and gave it to her.*

Chase looked around his yard and had an idea. He pulled out his phone and glanced at the time. He had just enough time to get to the hardware store and grab a shower before he needed to be back to the spa.

40

Ruby

Ruby got to Chase's house right at seven thirty. He opened the door with a grin, hugged her and kissed her slowly on the cheek. *Well, that all felt beyond wonderful.*

"Welcome. Clearly the dogs are also glad you're here." Hershey and Tuck were pushing their way between them to greet Ruby.

"I'm glad to see you too, pups." She bent to scratch them behind the ears, then followed Chase to the kitchen. "It smells amazing in here. And also, I'm beginning to feel guilty for all the meals. Maybe I can cook for you next time?"

"You don't need to feel guilty, but I'd love that," Chase said, pulling out the warmed tortillas. "I wasn't sure if you preferred hard or soft shells, so I did both. I also did both beef and chicken, so you can have your pick."

"I love it all, and I made sure to come really hungry because based on your previous cooking, I'm going to want to eat a lot."

Chase laughed. "You might want to save a little space. I have a special dessert planned."

"Ooooo. What is it?"

"You'll have to wait and see."

· · · • · • · · · ·

"I'm not sure I saved room for dessert," Ruby said, leaning back from the table. "Tacos are dangerous. There always seems to be space for another until there really isn't. And I've never had Spanish rice like that. I lost control. Your cooking made me lose control, Chase." She play-smacked his arm.

Chase smiled and laughed. "We don't have to eat dessert right away. Do me a favor and stay in here for a few—I need to step outside. Don't look out the window, okay?"

"Now I really want to look out the window when you leave."

Chase gave her a playfully stern look.

"I won't! I just said I want to!"

"I'll be back for you in a few minutes. Also, don't clean up. I'm going to stick the leftovers in the fridge, but I'll take care of the rest later. Just relax."

After dealing with the leftovers, Chase left and Ruby was up instantly to continue the cleaning. "Sorry, Chase." Only a few short minutes into her cleaning spree, she heard him heading back inside. Ruby rushed back to the table and acted like she had spent the time relaxing. He didn't seem to notice what she had been up to when he came into the room. *How can he not notice the difference?* She laughed to herself, then realized the answer. *All his focus is on me.*

"Are ya ready?"

"Yep!" she said with more strength than she was feeling. *But what I'm ready for, I'm not sure.*

He held out his hand, and taking it, she felt her peace return. Things were easy with Chase—she was the one always making it difficult. *Why do I have to be like this? Idiot Ethan. And couldn't my family and school move here?*

He led her out the screened porch door and into the dark, around to the backyard. Ruby gasped. "It's beautiful." *And we're still holding hands. I love it.* She hadn't realized she was so into hand-holding.

Chase had strung lights across the space between the house and two large maple trees. There was a small fire going in a firepit and a table holding a vase of small blue and white flowers along with the makings of s'mores.

"Is this what you meant by dessert?"

"I guess so." Chase gave her a crooked smile. "It's sort of an elaborate dessert tonight."

"This is amazing, but I'm afraid it's too much for someone who's leaving soon." The sadness was obvious in her voice, but she didn't care. Her emotions were overcoming her.

"I've decided to just do what I would do if you weren't leaving. I know you are, don't worry. But I wanted to do this for you, so I did. And really things just sort of spiraled out of control once I decided to do s'mores. Before I knew it, I was climbing trees, hanging lights."

"You're too good to me."

"Definitely not," Chase said, releasing her hand and pulling his phone from his pocket. "I had one other thing in mind for us to do, so maybe we can do that until you're ready for dessert." *Is kissing what he had in mind? I've certainly got it on* my *mind.*

"Amazed" began playing from his phone's speaker. "Since you're leaving before the next dance, I thought I would ask you to dance tonight. Do you think I should?"

Ruby could feel anticipation like lightning around her body. "You probably should." Her voice came out as a whisper.

"Beautiful Ruby, may I have this dance?"

She nodded, stepping forward and into his arms. "I do wonder why you chose a country song for our first dance."

"So you're saying you'd like there to be more dances?"

"We might dance twice tonight. You never know." Ruby grinned, thankful for a playful break in this otherwise serious moment.

Chase smiled into her hair. "I chose this song because you looked so pretty singing it on the night of the dance. And to be honest, I'm a bit amazed by you."

Oh, Chase. This would all be better than a dream if I didn't know it was finite. She buried her face into his chest, not knowing what to say or do, so she just stayed there swaying and feeling her time with him slipping away.

When "Amazed" drew to a close, she prepared to step away, but "Lovely Day" started to play. "You remember this? From the day we drove to get the picnic table." Chase picked up the pace and pep of their dance.

"I do," Ruby said with a laugh. "It was the first time I had a positive thought about you."

"Wow. You'd met my dogs by then, so surely that's not true," Chase said, pulling back to look at her.

"Maybe not, but it's the first one I remember strongly."

He smiled down at her then. The music and twinkling lights surrounded them as they held on to one another and swayed. When the song ended, another began, but Ruby took no notice of what it was because Chase spoke softly into her hair.

"I'd really like to kiss you again." He leaned back, gazing at her with stars in his eyes. Or perhaps it was just a reflection from the lights around them.

"I'd really like that too." All protestations had gotten lost in her throat. They weren't even in her mind as he held her and looked at her with those stormy blue eyes. She reached up and twirled one of his black curls around her finger, then brought her hand to his jaw. "Kiss me now, Chase."

He kept one hand on her back and the other moved to the back of her hair. He cut the distance between their lips in half and said, "It would be my pleasure." He cut the distance once more and added, "And hopefully yours."

Ruby couldn't help herself. She pushed up on her toes and kissed him with a ferocity that surprised her. Chase lifted her off her feet and held her as they continued to sway to the music. Their hearts were aligned in more ways than one, it seemed. *How am I ever going to leave this place? Leave him?*

She stopped kissing him for a moment so she could look at his face. Memorize it. *There's something incredibly special about him. I don't want to break his heart. Or mine.* She held back tears as she kissed him again, slower this time, threading her fingers through the back of his hair. Chase adjusted his hold on her. The way he was kissing her, the intensity and heat coming off him were almost overwhelming.

Ruby could feel the pounding of his heart and his hard, heavy breathing. He nuzzled into her neck and cheek. "I could do this forever," he whispered into her ear.

I could too. But we need to calm down now. I'm already in too deep.

"Eventually your arms would get tired and you'd have to put me down," she whispered back. "Or someone would need to pee."

· · · · **·** · **·** · · ·

They moved on to dessert, where Ruby learned with outrage that Chase preferred his marshmallows burnt.

"How is that *not* like eating charcoal?" she asked with an exaggerated look of disgust on her face.

"It's not like the inside is hard. In fact, the inside is perfect."

"But the flavor of the outside is like smoke meets rocks meets sugar."

He choked on a laugh. "Let's just agree to disagree."

"Never. But we can stop talking about it. For now."

Chase sighed and smiled, squeezing his black marshmallow and chocolate between his graham crackers.

"I'm not sure you can kiss me again tonight with burnt rocks mouth."

"I thought we were finished with the burnt marshmallow hate."

"Okay. Okay. I'm finished now...maybe."

After dessert, Ruby decided it was probably best if she headed back to the bakery. She looked around the yard, knowing this had been a night she wouldn't soon, or perhaps ever, forget. She didn't want to fall further for him. Or lead him on more than she already had. *This is such a mess. Or maybe I'm a mess. Who am I kidding? That's definitely true, Ethan saw to that.* She decided it was probably best if they didn't kiss again when she left.

Chase walked with Ruby to her car, holding her hand. He had grabbed it like it was an old habit, threading their fingers as if he had done it a thousand times. *I love the feeling of his hand. Strong but soft, all those massage lotions and oils leaving silky skin behind.* Lost in her reverie about his hands, Ruby didn't notice Chase turning and leaning in once they reached her car. Their kiss was sweet and tender, sending a shiver down her spine. Ruby pulled back slightly and said into his lips, "You're really good at this."

He bit her lower lip while smiling, then released it and said, "Only because it's you."

41

Chase

CHASE DIDN'T KNOW HOW he was going to do it. He woke before the sun, feeling terribly unsettled. He had told her he would be fine, that he would deal with her disappearance later, but he was already feeling it. He had less than two weeks left with her, and if things continued as they were, his heart would be a shredded, unrecognizable mess when she was gone. Treating her like there was a chance might have been a terrible mistake. The overwhelming depth of his feelings last night made it clear what he would be losing. It was literally painful when he released her from his arms and watched her go. *What am I doing to myself?*

Chase was on autopilot, lost in a jumble of thoughts, as he prepared his breakfast and took care of Hershey and Tuck. He sat his smoothie in the freezer, deciding to take the dogs for a run and have it later. *Maybe I'll feel better after a run.*

He took the dogs out on the trails, preferring likely solitude to the possibility of running into someone on the streets of town. At first their run was all about speed and attempting to force the anxiety from his body. Eventually he slowed to a jog. He found a bit of peace in the beauty of his surroundings, the morning light filtering through the trees, the songbirds singing their sunrise melodies. He held on to that peace until his eyes landed on a particularly vivid patch of moss that reminded him of those beautiful green eyes. The sight filled him with both love and dread. He loved her. He actually loved her after thinking he would never let himself, or perhaps never be truly capable of it.

Chase led the dogs off the trail and into a small clearing. He unclipped their leashes so they could sniff and play as they'd like and he lay down in the sun. Whether from the exercise-induced endorphins or the sunshine, he didn't know, but he instantly felt better.

He lay, taking deep breaths of soothing forest air, making decisions and plans. *It's not over for us, because she's it for me. I know it.*

Chase had a renewed sense of purpose and certainly a better outlook on the situation when he and his dogs emerged from the woods. He showered, grabbed his smoothie and headed for work. He had a rather full day of massages, which was probably best for a day like this one. It would certainly stop Chase from simply showing up at the bakery to sit and stare at Ruby. *No good could come from that anyway.*

· · • • · • • · · ·

When Chase came out from his two o'clock massage, he was beginning to tire and was looking forward to a much-needed break before his 3:45. He checked his phone on the way to the break room. There was a text waiting from Ruby. His heart smiled.

> **Green-eyed Ruby:** Mamu and I stopped by on the way out of town so I could say goodbye, but you had just gone into a massage. My brother had an accident during police training and we're rushing home. I don't think I'll be back. Our time together was incredible and I'll never forget it. I'm sorry to have to say goodbye in this way. I'll miss you.

And just like that, the world stopped spinning.

· · • • · • • · ·

What is the role of a friend who wants to be way more than that when the brother of the girl he loves is in a maybe-life-or-death situation? She clearly didn't expect anything, but did she need him? She'd have her parents and grandmother. If he were to show up like he would like to, it might add a layer of stress that wouldn't be helpful. But what if she would actually love for him to be there? It seemed to Chase like it could go either way.

He had an extremely difficult time making it through his last massage, making sure the client got the experience he deserved. He was heavily booked at the spa over the following days, so he decided to stay put and see how things went with Ruby. To text her and try to stay in contact.

He waited until he got home to have a chance to clear his mind before texting Ruby. He grabbed a drink and sat on his sofa.

> **Chase:** I'm so sorry to hear about your brother's accident. How is he doing? How are you?
>
> **Chase:** I'll miss you too. So much.

Maybe I shouldn't have added the "so much." Too late now. It's true, though.

> **Green-eyed Ruby:** I haven't gotten an update from my parents lately, but apparently he was out doing some on-site training when a person floored the gas and drove up onto the sidewalk. He was hit and thrown through the glass of the boutique they were standing in front of. There was so much bleeding and internal damage. He was in surgery when I last heard.
>
> **Chase:** That's horrible. Please let me know how the surgery goes. Is there anything I can do?

Should I offer to come? No, that might freak her out more.

> **Green-eyed Ruby:** I'll do my best to remember. I don't think so, but thanks. We're almost to the hos-

pital, so hopefully I will have an update soon.

Chase: I hope he's ok, Ruby. *Red heart emoji*

There was no response. Chase leaned his head on the back of the sofa and closed his eyes, feeling a bit guilty for thinking so much about how this situation affected him.

42

Ruby

RUBY AND MAMU BURST through the doors to the hospital. They approached the front desk, where a middle-aged woman wearing cat-eye glasses and a French twist sat using a computer. "Hello," Mamu said loudly, still not anywhere near the desk. "We're looking for my grandson, Charles Alan Butler. How can we find him?"

"Hello, ma'am, miss." The woman smiled at them genially. "I'll look on the computer, and while I'm doing that, please get out your IDs and so I can make visitors badges."

After retrieving her license, Ruby looked at the items on the desk. There was a stack of papers to nominate a staff member for exceptionally caring service. The papers had a big red heart on them, which reminded her of Chase's last text. *What did that heart mean? That he cares? That he loves me? Ugh, now is not the time for this.* The woman was moving at a maddeningly slow pace, but her calming presence soothed Ruby as they were held up at this last step before reaching her brother.

Eventually, with sticker IDs on their shirts, Mamu and Ruby followed the directions given to them and made it to surgery waiting. At the first sight of her parents, both Mamu and Ruby stopped in their tracks. Ruby wasn't sure how to interpret what she was seeing. Her mother was sitting with her face in her hands while her father, sitting beside her, rested his head on her shoulder and rubbed a hand up and down her back. It looked like devastation. Had he died in surgery? Had she missed the last weeks of her brother's life while she was in Maine, fooling around? Or maybe they were just lost in their worry? *Deep breaths, Ruby.*

She and Mamu looked at each other as if gathering strength and entered the room. "Mom. Dad." Her parents looked up, giving her weak smiles and rising. Ruby filled with relief. She knew there would be no smiles, even weak ones, if he were gone.

"What's going on? How is he?" Ruby asked, hugging each of her parents. "Have you seen him at all?"

"We haven't been able to see him," Nichole said, sitting back down.

"He was in surgery when we got here," Jared added. "That finished a couple hours ago and we were told it went well and we were hoping to see him before long, but then a nurse showed up and told us they had to take him into another surgery. We're expecting an update anytime."

They sat in silence, nobody really knowing what to say as they waited. It was, thankfully, only ten minutes later that they saw a doctor heading their direction. She walked right to Ruby's parents. Obviously she had seen them before.

"Mr. and Mrs. Butler," the doctor said, nodding to Jared and Nichole.

Ruby's father spoke. "This is Ruby, Charlie's sister. And my mother, Amelia."

"Nice to meet you both, I'm Dr. Marayna Ahn. Charlie came out of surgery half an hour ago and is in recovery. His bleeding is under control and I expect him to make a full recovery. I'm afraid it will be a long recovery, but he's young and it seems he was in excellent health before, so I expect he will do well."

The collective breath was released as she informed them of his successful surgery. Ruby was filled with relief, followed quickly by anxiety about his recovery period and what she could do to help. *Charlie is all that matters right now. I can't believe we almost lost him. I'm going to make sure he recovers well and quickly.*

· · · • · • · · ·

Late that evening, they were finally able to see Charlie. As she looked down at him in his hospital bed, Ruby wasn't sure she would recognize him if she didn't know who he was. His face was puffy and covered with stitched areas and abrasions. *That's my brother. Oh my gosh, that's my brother in there.*

At the noise of their entrance, Charlie opened his eyes to minuscule slits. "Hey," he croaked from the bed. "Fancy seeing you here."

The surprised laughter filling the room was infused with relief. "Oh, Charlie!" his mother said with a huge sigh, approaching the bed. Ruby was a bit afraid she was going to fling herself onto the bed, crushing Charlie in her relief. *I'm watching you, Mom.*

Charlie gave his mother the best smile he could manage. "I'm going to be fine, Mom. You can relax."

"Can I hold your hand?" Nichole asked.

"I'll allow it."

She sighed and smiled. "I mean, are you hurt there?"

"As far as I know, it's fine."

Ruby, Jared and Mamu each spoke briefly with Charlie before he said he needed to sleep again.

"I'll stay here if the rest of you would like to go home and get some sleep," Ruby offered, knowing she was the only one among them who stood a chance of actually sleeping on that thinly covered piece of plywood that somehow passed as a recliner.

Nichole started to protest, but Jared stepped in. "You need rest. We can come back first thing in the morning. Yeah? Ruby will call us right away if we need to get here."

"Of course I will. But there'll be no need. Just healing and recovery happening in this room!" Ruby was stressed but hoped her positive words came across as genuine.

"Okay," Nichole agreed. "But I want to go get some things and stay at that hotel across the street so we're close by. Millie, want to stay with us?"

"Yes, I'd like to stay close too," Mamu said, turning to look at Charlie. "Sweet boy, we'll see you in the morning."

· · • ·•·•· · · ·

Ruby settled into her chair as best she could. It had been an incredibly long day. She grabbed her phone to message her parents that all was well but decided not to in case they were already asleep. She imagined they were well past exhaustion and fell asleep before their heads even hit their pillows. While she had her phone, however, she did see someone else she needed to text. *I don't need to be thinking about Chase. I need to focus on Charlie.* But he had asked for an update, and she didn't want him to be left wondering.

> **Ruby:** Hey, Chase. Charlie is doing ok. He had two surgeries, but he's expected to be fine. Will be a long recovery.

Three dots appeared almost instantly. Chase was there and she could feel herself getting excited just by this connection. *What am I doing? I have got to leave him behind me.*

> **Chase:** Hey, Bee. I'm so relieved! How are you doing?
> **Ruby:** I'm ok. Just tired. I'm staying at the hospital tonight. Going to go now and try to get some sleep in this horrendous excuse for a chair.
> **Chase:** Glad you're ok. I hope you get some shockingly good sleep. You never know!
> **Ruby:** Thanks. We'll see. Goodnight.
> **Chase:** Nite *Bee Emoji*

43

Chase

CHASE MISSED RUBY TERRIBLY and felt the distance between them more viscerally than he would have expected. He was in bed, unable to sleep. Wishing there had been more to the texting with Ruby. What had he been expecting? *Her mind is on her brother, as it should be.* Chase sighed. *I just wish I had had more time to make sure she thinks of me and misses me when the time is right. I don't know if she will.*

Chase turned to lie on his stomach, the position making him wish he was getting a massage. He had been tense all day. He needed to be proactive. *How can I eventually come back to her mind?* His thoughts ranged from useless to silly until he remembered something Ruby had told him. *There's an art gallery where she lives.* He decided to go see Mr. Kishlar after work the next day. *I'll get in that gallery, so if nothing else, I'll see her when I'm there.*

· · • • · • · • • · · ·

When Chase arrived at Mr. Kishlar's, he found him reading in his garden. Ryan had developed a particular fondness for cozy mysteries over the past couple of years.

"Hey. I was wondering if you could help me. I want to get into this art gallery. I have these paintings and a couple more I'm working on that I think will go nicely with them."

"Right to business, I see. It's nice to see you—you've been MIA recently."

"I met someone I was spending a lot of time with."

"Well, good. I was worried about you."

"You were *worried* about me?"

"I'm not without eyes or a heart, Chase. You obviously had some-thing going on, but I simply am not a friendship-type person. I did try to keep you busy so you weren't marinating in your sadness alone in that apartment."

Chase was stunned and more than a little touched. *All the land-scaping and fixing of things.* "That seems a bit friend-like, Ryan."

"Don't get overexcited," Ryan said, leaving his book and standing. "Let's have a look at these paintings."

They walked to the easel, where Chase pulled out the paintings and displayed them one at a time. Ryan studied them with his ex-tremely critical eye, not saying a word, only indicating when he was ready for the next. *Say something, man, I can't stand this.*

When he finished his lengthy examination of the final painting, Ryan turned to Chase. "These are magnificent. You've found that extra something we were talking about a few weeks ago. There's more depth here. And more varied feeling. Your previous paintings were technically lovely, but consistently morose. Put the one of the falls back up—I want to talk about it."

· · · ● · ● · · · ·

Chase talked with Mr. Kishlar for hours, about the paintings, getting into the gallery and even a little about Ruby. Chase left feeling encouraged, with Ryan promising to call the gallery and put in a good word. In the meantime, Chase headed home to work on the other paintings he wished to take.

He hadn't heard from Ruby today and he itched to text her or maybe even call, but he didn't want to bother her. *Who knows, she might be sleeping, if sleep didn't happen for her last night.* He remembered when he was in middle school and his mom was briefly in the hospital. His dad came home with an aching back, saying, "Those chairs ain't worth a durn!"

He decided to call his dad because it had been a while since their last chat. His dad answered on the first ring.

"Hello there, Chase!"

"Hey, Dad. That was a quick answer. Were you sitting there waiting for me to call? It hasn't been *that* long since we've talked, has it?"

"I was playing Tetris. Did you know you can play Tetris on your phone? I'll show you next time we see you. Although it's not the same as playing it the old way. Still fun, though, still fun."

Chase shook his head. "I actually did know that. There are a lot of phone games out there. I don't have Tetris, though."

"Well, you should get it."

"Maybe I will."

"You're just saying that, I can tell." His dad chuckled. "But anyway, how are ya, son?"

"I'm doing good. I have some paintings hopefully going to a gallery soon, so that's pretty exciting."

"That's fantastic! Any we've seen?"

"No. These are all new. I'll be taking photos to send to the gallery, and I'll send them to you and Mom too."

"I can't wait to see them, Chase. I'm so proud of you. We both are."

"Thanks, Dad. I'm actually a little bit proud of me, too." Chase chuckled. "I can't wait for you to see them and hear what you guys think."

"What, honey?" Chase's dad called, his voice muffled. *I guess Mom's nearby.* "Your mom wants me to ask you what's happening with the girl you're friends with."

Mom, this is not why I called.

Chase gave his father the short version of what was going on, leaving out just how involved his heart had become.

"Well, bud, that's a tough spot. If y'all are meant to be, I don't believe it could be stopped. Just keep putting yourself out there. Be available and supportive. Give it some time, her life is obviously weird right now. Once things settle down for her a bit, go after her. Show her how you feel, lay it all out so the ball is in her court. And believe it or not, if things don't work out, if she doesn't run to you wanting the same, there will be someone else. Someone that feels so right and wonderful that you can't imagine your life any other way."

There's no way that's not Ruby. I can't imagine my life any other way than with her.

44

Ruby

CHARLIE SPENT NEARLY A week in the hospital, after which he had far too many home nurses and he was getting rather annoyed. "You guys have got to calm down. I don't need all this attention. At least come up with a plan. Take turns. I'm not extroverted enough for all this people time."

His family looked at him, appearing thoroughly chastised. "Okay, we'll come up with a plan," his mother said, patting his arm.

"I can stay during the day, until I have to get back to the classroom. And then after that, I can come after school."

"If I still need care by then," Charlie interjected.

They ignored him. "Your dad and I can just work together in the evenings, but not in an overwhelming way. But what about the night shift? I could get an air mattress in here…"

"That will not be necessary," Charlie said emphatically. "I have a phone, if I really needed to get you in the night."

"I could buy a baby monitor," Nichole said mostly to herself.

"Mom, I'm going to Carter's house to recover."

"Okay, okay. No mattress or baby monitor," his mother conceded.

"I'm going to go home and get out of the way," Ruby said. "But I'll be back after breakfast, okay?"

"Sounds good, sweetheart. See you in the morning." Ruby's mother kissed her cheek.

Ruby bent to gently hug her brother. "See ya tomorrow."

On the way down the porch steps, Ruby spotted Mamu heading her way. "Turn around, we're smothering him."

Mamu waited on Ruby and walked with her to the car. "Wanna go eat?"

"Yes, I really do," Ruby said with a grin. "I'm so tired of hospital food and the stuff those certainly very nice people brought over."

"No casseroles or mediocre hamburgers, got it. I know just the place for us."

· · · • · • · • · · ·

Ruby didn't know what day it was. The whirlwind of their exodus from Maine combined with the time at the hospital had left her drained and unaware of anything going on outside of her immediate surroundings. Mamu had dropped her off at her apartment after dinner and she decided she was past due for some Ruby time. She started a bath, put on a face mask and settled into the water with her current novel. A murder mystery—not her typical genre, but Vera had convinced her she had to give it a try.

At a particularly suspenseful moment, her phone buzzed. Ruby almost dropped her book in the tub. She gave her heart a few seconds to settle, then she set her book aside, grabbing her phone.

> **Chase:** Hey, Bee. I was just hiking with Hersh and Tuck near Laurel Falls (the falls) and I saw some people coming out from the falls. It made me think of you. I hope you're doing well. How's Charlie?
> **Ruby:** He's recovering slowly but surely. He's getting cranky, which I'm taking as a good sign. I'm doing okay. Settling in back in my apartment, adjusting to a new schedule of helping Charlie and preparing to go back to school.

I'm gone, Chase. Remember that and accept it. Ruby felt a tear sliding down her cheek.

> **Chase:** Don't forget to take care of yourself.
> **Ruby:** I won't. I'm taking a relaxing bath right now.

Why did I have to say that? I could have easily just left it at "I won't." Now I've planted the idea of me in the bathtub into his head, which I'm certain he doesn't need. Ruby!

> **Chase:** Oh. I don't want to bother you during relaxing bath time.

You're not. Ruby sighed, feeling another tear. *It's better this way.* Her family needed her and she'd be starting work soon. She had to move on. And so did he.

Ruby: No worries.
Chase: Enjoy yourself. I'll catch ya later.

I don't think you will, Chase. We've got to let each other go.

45

Chase

CHASE THREW HIMSELF INTO completing his final paintings and planning what he would finally say when he saw Ruby again. The thought of her motivated every brushstroke, every color he mixed with care. She inspired and moved him, every memory and kernel of contact moving him forward.

As he worked and planned, however, his texts with Ruby became less and less satisfying. And more and more troubling.

One week apart:

> **Chase:** I ran into Gerald today. He said Ms. Millie is coming back in a day or two. It will be good to see her, but I'm sure you'll miss her.
> **Ruby:** I will. It's been good having her here to help.
> **Chase:** I bet. I think she has more energy than most people half her age.

Chase: *Energizer Bunny gif*

Ruby: You're right about that!

Three weeks apart:

Chase: How's your brother?

Ruby: He's up and walking around some, but still needs a lot of help. I go after school for my nursing shift.

Chase: I'm so glad he's up and moving. I bet that will increase his healing exponentially.

Ruby: I hope so.

Chase: How's school?

Ruby: Going well so far.

Chase: Well, good. I miss you.

One month apart:

Chase: I saw Ms. Millie this morning. She has information on the man we saw having the yacht party at the lake!

Ruby: I'm actually seeing her tonight at my parents'. I'll have to ask.

Two months apart:

Chase: Hey. How's Charlie? How's school?

Ten weeks apart:

Chase: Hey *bee emoji*

She's shut me out. He scrolled back through all the texts from after she'd left. It didn't take long, given how few there were. He had always been the one to initiate the texting, apart from the first update about Charlie. She responded either with the bare minimum or not at all. Why was she doing this?

Chase cleaned up his painting space and headed to shower. He stood with his forehead and raised arms against the wall, letting the water beat against his back. *Is this what I get for opening up again?* He pounded the wall with his fist. *Do I not get to have people to love? A best friend brother. The girl who I thought was the love of my life.* He hit the wall again. *We could have worked this out. Why is she doing this? We had something, I know we did.*

Chase finished his shower and stormed to the screened porch. He took his latest, nearly complete painting, tore it off the frame and ripped the canvas in two. Regret instantly infused his system. The ruined painting had been his best work to date. One he could never recreate, should he ever have the desire to try.

· · · ● · ● · · ·

Chase woke late the next day, the sun streaming through blinds he had neglected to close the night before. His eyes were puffy from the tears of anger and the tears of pain he let out as he tossed and turned in bed.

His stomach growled in protest of his staying in bed any longer. *I need to get out of here. Be around some people.* He decided to go to the diner. He hadn't been there at all since Ruby showed up.

He drove to the diner only to find a sign on the door saying they were closed due to a plumbing emergency. It was a beautiful sunny morning, so he decided to walk down Main Street to a little place that served breakfast sandwiches. That was, however, not where he found himself.

The bell jingled as he opened the door and stepped into The Sweet Spot Bakery. Ms. Millie looked up from where she was sliding muffins into the display case.

"Chase. How wonderful to see you. I've missed you lately. Would you like a muffin?" She pulled one out without waiting for an answer. "It's blueberry with a strudel topping."

"Thanks, Ms. Millie, I am pretty hungry. I've missed you too. How are you?" Chase took the plate with a smile and followed Ms. Millie's lead to a booth against the wall.

"Can't complain. How about you? It's been too long. I'm sorry I haven't checked in."

"Don't worry about it. I've mostly been painting and working. I'm okay."

"I'm glad to hear that."

Chase took a bite of his muffin and smiled. "This is delicious. I can't believe you didn't go to baking school or whatever."

"I have learned a lot over the years. Baking wisdom, I guess. Plus, I enjoy it, so that helps too."

"How's Ruby?" Chase tried to seem less interested in the answer than he really was. Like it wasn't all he ever wanted to know.

"School's going well. Charlie's requiring a little less help these days, so she has some more free time. That's good for her, I think."

Chase simply nodded. Ms. Millie reached over the table and rubbed his arm.

"I'm really sorry for how things ended with you guys. I thought you had something special."

"Me too. Is she... dating anyone?"

Ms. Millie removed her hand from his arm, looking at him with sympathy. "She isn't. Although, she did go on a date last week. It went terribly from what I heard."

Chase felt shattered and encouraged at the same time. He couldn't believe she felt ready to go on a date. *I wonder if it went badly because she remembered me and he didn't compare. Let's say that's the case.*

As he left the bakery, Chase was ecstatic to get a phone call from the gallery in Vermont. Mr. Kishlar had really come through for him. *This is really happening!* They asked him to send photos, so they could confirm all Mr. Kishlar's praise and make a plan for the exhibit. If all went well, he would be in Vermont in a month. *At least I can sell some paintings, even if the dream of Ruby is dead.*

48

Ruby

BETWEEN SCHOOL AND HELPING her brother, Ruby hardly had time to breathe. She seldom thought of Chase, and when she did, she didn't know if it was a good thing or not. She was so caught up in everything else. Ruby saw his texts come in and either didn't have a chance to answer or didn't have the time or brain capacity to respond as she should.

He would often come to mind at night in the moments before her tired body succumbed to sleep. She felt guilty, knowing how Chase must be feeling. Her heartbreak was masked by activity, but deep down, she knew it was there. *This is for the best, though. For both of us. I think.*

Ruby sat at her desk in her classroom, grading the first tests of the semester, eyes threatening to close. She opened her bottom drawer and grabbed a piece of her emergency caramel dark chocolate, needing a boost to finish up. She was pulling on her sweater when her coworker, fellow math teacher Olivia Parker, walked in.

"I want to set you up with my boyfriend's best friend, Jay. We can go on double dates. Wouldn't that be fun!?"

"I really don't have time for anything else right now." *And I'm really not ready.*

"Maybe once Charlie's doing better? Yeah?"

"Yeah, maybe then."

· · · • · • · · · ·

Ruby sat in the restaurant waiting for her date, wondering how she had ended up there. Olivia was some sort of wordsmith wizard, beginning with "How is your brother?" and leading up to "It's been a month since I tried to set you up with Jay, and since Charlie is doing much better—"

"Dang you, Olivia," Ruby muttered under her breath as she watched the time on her phone tick over to 7:12. *At least twelve minutes late. Strike one.*

Several minutes later, Ruby watched as a moderately attractive man carrying a small bouquet of flowers entered the restaurant. He spoke with the hostess, who indicated toward Ruby, and Ruby sighed. She had very much hoped she was being stood up.

As Jay approached, Ruby stood to shake his hand. Instead, he hugged her, kissed her cheek and shoved the flowers into her hand. *Strike two.*

"Olivia said you were beautiful, but dayum, she undersold you."

Jay sat as Ruby stared down at him in shock. She considered leaving, but she was extremely excited for the salmon she planned to order. She'd heard it was delicious.

·•·•●·●•·•·

"Got time to chat?"

"Sure thing. I'm just getting in from work," Vera said on the other end of the line.

"This late?"

"Work emergency."

"Seems like there's always an emergency."

"You're telling me. So what's up? You're using your 'I'm aggravated' voice."

Ruby rolled her eyes and smiled at how well her friend knew her. "I let a coworker set me up and it was awful. On the bright side, the food was delicious."

"Of course it was awful. It wasn't Chase."

"Vera, that's not helpful."

"Okay, okay. I'm sorry. It's just that guys like him don't come around every day. I hate to think of you missing out. I feel like I have second-degree heartbreak from this."

Ruby sighed. "It just didn't work out. Logistically it didn't make sense. I guess I did decide I could trust him, but when it came down to it, I live here. My family is here, you're close by. Charlie needs me even when he's not sick."

"Poor thing is a little bit like a helpless puppy sometimes." Vera laughed, then continued. "But your parents are here for him too, you know. You're not the only one who can do things. And also, when the time comes, I should be the only one allowed to set you up."

"Lesson learned. I really like Olivia, but she wasted her one shot."

"I'd never do that to you."

"I know."

. . . .

Ruby spent the next several days preparing first-quarter progress reports and scrubbing her date with Jay and the subsequent thoughts of Chase from her mind. She closed her school laptop and set it on the sofa beside her. She was heading to her room to get ready for bed when there was a knock on her door. She wasn't expecting anyone, so she went to look out the peephole. *Charlie.*

"Hey." Charlie walked in like he lived there and plopped down on the sofa.

"My laptop!"

"Oh, sorry about that." He pulled the computer out from underneath his leg and sat it on the coffee table. "You really shouldn't leave a laptop somewhere it could be sat on."

"Well, I knew *I* wasn't going to be flopping down on top of it. What are you doing here?"

"Rude."

"Sorry, I'm ready to go to sleep."

"I need you to convince Mom and Dad that I'm well enough to have some space. I had to sneak out to get here. They are driving me insane—I mean, the doctor said I recovered twice as fast as they expected. He cleared me to drive and do normal things, but I can't make them believe I'm okay. I need less help. I've been looking at apartments I can afford until I can get back to the academy and then actually work."

"I'll see what I can do. I can't believe they can't see how much better you're doing."

"I can. They treated me like a child, even before the accident. I grew up and nobody noticed."

"Keep showing them, they'll see it."

"I hope so." Charlie shifted to get more comfortable.

I need to go to sleep, Charlie.

"Hey, are you doing okay?" he asked, eyes closed. "I've been meaning to ask."

"I'm fine."

"Are you sure? You seem off. At first I thought it was my accident, but it's been three months now and I'm obviously okay, so it must be something else."

How shockingly perceptive for my little brother.

"You're right, I've not been myself, but I'll be back to normal before too long." *Maybe.*

47

CHASE KNEW HIS FINAL two paintings for the show were by far the best he had ever done. Even better than the one he had, regretfully, torn apart. He carefully packaged and shipped his work to the gallery. The anticipation of seeing them there, mixed with the crumbs of hope he still held on to that he might see Ruby, was almost too much. Time moved so very slowly.

By the time Chase was packing his bag and loading his car, he was feeling a bit numb to his situation. The drive to Vermont dragged and was devoid of the excitement he had previously felt. Everything had soured and he would be lying if he said he wasn't a little ticked that his first gallery showing was tainted in that way.

Driving through the town, he noticed that while it was certainly much larger than Laurel Falls, it was no less charming. *I can see why she would want to come back here. What does Laurel Falls have that this place doesn't? Besides me and her grandmother, of course.*

Chase parked on Main Street, in front of Babbo Italian Kitchen, across the street from Belles Oeuvres d'Art. He sighed, gazing across the street. *I can salvage this. This is going to be good.*

There was a sign displayed by the door, advertising the show. He looked down at his face and name and his heart was filled with gratitude and a sense of accomplishment like he had not previously felt. He stepped into the gallery and there was a lone man standing behind a table, busily working on something. He hadn't noticed Chase's entrance.

"*Merde!*" the man exclaimed as he looked up, obviously very surprised to see someone standing there. "*Pardonnez-moi*, I am very sorry. I had in my earbuds and I did not hear you come in. I am Amédée Lavigne." The man reached for Chase's hand.

"Very nice to meet you, I'm Chase—"

"I know who you are, Chase Davidson," Mr. Lavigne interrupted. "Look at that face. Pardon my saying, but I think we would have a packed gallery with just a photo of you."

Chase laughed awkwardly, not knowing how to respond.

"The sign looks great." Chase smiled, indicating back toward the door. "How long have you been in the US?" he asked, hoping to change the subject from his beautiful face.

"I moved here almost eleven years ago. I met my wife when she was studying in France as an exchange student. She lived here and didn't want to leave her family. I told her I would follow her wherever she wanted to go. So here I am. Best decision I ever made."

Well, that sounds oddly familiar. Chase wanted to make that decision too. He had previously been determined to abandon his plan to reconnect with Ruby while in town. He decided he would give it a shot. He would text her before heading to the hotel and see what happened.

"She must be special to come all the way from France."

"Special is the least of it."

Chase smiled, glancing back to the sign with his photo. "I can't believe this is really happening."

"Believe it, Chase. We are honored to have you and help launch you into the world. I'm afraid you are so good, we will never have another of your pieces come through *this* gallery."

Chase was extremely touched and surprised. "I appreciate that so much. And you never know, this place is already very special to me."

"Here's hoping." Mr. Lavigne clapped his hands once, excited. "Come, Chase. I can't wait for you to see your work displayed."

· · · • · • · · · ·

Mr. Lavigne certainly had an eye for setting up the exhibit in a way that moved and flowed. Art on its own without distracting from the paintings. "This looks great, Mr. Lavigne."

"Amédée, please," he said, clearly admiring the space. "Yes, it is perfect. Your work will shine. Show starts at seven if you'd like to go to your hotel and get ready. I'll have everything else ready to go by then."

"Sounds good, yeah. I'll see you then. And thanks for everything, Amédée."

"Of course, Chase. Thank *you* and thank Ryan Kishlar. This is going to be spectacular."

Chase walked to his car encouraged and excited. He decided to go ahead and text Ruby. He hoped the positive experiences would keep rolling in.

Chase: Hey, Ruby. What are you up to?

If she answers, I'll invite her. If not, I'd rather she not even know I was here.

48

Ruby

RUBY WAS ROLLING MEATBALLS for the spaghetti she was making for her family when she felt her phone buzz in her pocket. *I'll get that later.*

Her phone remained in her pocket, however, as she continued cooking dinner and then enjoyed the meal with her family. She got another notification in her pocket on her way home that evening and waited until she got into her apartment to pull out her phone. The most recent was a man her friend Morgan had set her up with confirming their dinner plans for the following night (*why did I agree to do this again?*), but the one from earlier was from Chase.

To hear from him was a shock to say the least. After all this time, she'd thought she'd never be in contact with him again. *What am I up to? Oh, Chase. I told you we were finite.* In the past months, she had been able to largely block Chase from her mind. The memories hurt too much. When they did sneak into her mind, she was always thrown for a loop, and getting this text was absolutely heartbreaking. Not only did it break for her, but it also broke for Chase. Not for the first time she questioned her choices, her guilt resurfacing with a vengeance.

It had already been a few hours since he'd messaged. She decided she might as well wait until tomorrow to respond. She didn't know what to say. *Maybe I'll figure something out by then.*

Ruby put her phone down, knowing she had to do something about this the next day. She couldn't let Chase hope for nothing. Ruby felt like there was a storm cloud hovering over her all evening and she woke the next morning feeling much the same. She decided to be simple with her response, saying the only thing she knew to say.

Ruby: I'm so sorry, Chase.

She didn't hear back.

· · · · ●· ● · · · ·

Being that it was Saturday, Ruby had planned to relax and, if she felt like it, do some things around her apartment. Relaxing, however, was not something Ruby did that day. Dark clouds continued to mound above her as she stressed in heartache about what to do about Chase. She was surprised he ignored her, but she couldn't say she blamed him. She almost canceled her dinner date but didn't want to be rude and didn't want to hurt her friend who'd set them up. *Who knows? I could be pleasantly surprised. Can't be worse than Jay, at any rate.*

She met her date, Tobias, at Babbo Italian Kitchen downtown. Ruby parked on Main Street and walked in a fog to the restaurant. The food was excellent, but the date left a lot to be desired. Tobias was extremely pretentious, which was saying something because Ruby was self-aware enough to know she was a bit pretentious herself. He was also self-centered, spending seventy-five percent of the time talking about the business he'd started and how much hotter he had gotten since high school. He paid for dinner, which, honestly, Ruby thought was the least he could do after her having to sit through an infomercial for the guy the whole time. He, of course, proved to be a terrible tipper. She slipped a few dollars on the table when he wasn't looking. Tobias was an obvious no-go and Ruby was beginning to question if her friends were actually friends at all.

It was a beautiful, unseasonably warm October evening, the light breeze only hinting at fall, so Ruby decided to try and salvage things with a walk around Main Street before heading home.

Downtown hadn't always been a place to hang around, to shop and eat, but recent years had brought all sorts of nice additions to her little town. A variety of restaurants and boutiques, a cute bookstore and even the century-old hardware store had been revitalized, making the area a place locals and tourists alike flocked to. Ruby remembered telling Chase about the art gallery when she saw the sign for it in the distance. As she walked past, she did a double take at the sign by the door. *Chase.* She stood staring at the sign, her thoughts silent as she looked at that face she loved. *Love. Do I love him? Surely that's not what I'm feeling.*

Ruby read the sign, then stared at his picture once again. *Is he in there? Do artists attend their shows? This is why he texted—his show started last night.* She walked in looking for him, but when she didn't see him, she headed in the direction of his paintings. She stopped at the first and was absolutely floored. She recognized the scene. It was from the night they had been hit by the moose. The sunset coming through the trees was breathtaking, but she couldn't stop staring at the two figures, barely discernible, walking in the shadows.

Ruby's heart was pounding as she approached the next painting. She found a simple woods scene with an ax leaned against a pile of logs. She was immediately taken back to the day she'd completely embarrassed herself after she'd spied him chopping wood. She moved on to the next and gasped. It was Laurel Falls, the falls. *This is the most beautiful painting I've ever seen. Chase is so unbelievably gifted.* Ruby couldn't take her eyes off the painting, imagining them in the scene. Remembering his eyes upon her when she entered the water and the look of terror, then relief when she came up from the water.

When she finally moved on, she was met with a close-up painting of mountain laurel in bloom. Chase's favorite flower. *Gorgeous.* The next was a painting much like the one he had done for her, only this one was zoomed out farther and had a canoe with oars floating unmanned near the shore. This whole show. Every single painting. It was memories of their time together. *I can't believe this. What have I done? I've been an idiot. An absolute fool.*

Ruby moved on to the next and saw the barn from the dance, surrounded by gently rolling hills. The next was a bright moon over trees and a house shaped much like Chase's. *That's the night we kissed the first time. The moon was so bright and gorgeous that night. That night. One of the best of my life.*

Overwhelmed, she sat on a bench that had been set up for viewing the work. *Oh, Chase. Chase. He could be here!* She had forgotten, with all the overwhelming feelings the paintings evoked. She hopped up and searched the small gallery. Chase was nowhere to be seen. Ruby, afraid she was looking frantic, calmed down and looked for an employee. She found a man and waited for him to finish speaking to a couple who had just walked in.

"Hello, mademoiselle, how can I help you?"

"Hi. The artist, Chase Davidson. Is he here?"

"I'm afraid not. He was meant to be here yesterday and today, but he decided to go back home this morning. He is a delightful young man, though. I hate you missed him."

"Me too," Ruby said in a near whisper. "Thank you for your help."

She left the gallery and walked to her car. She started up but just sat there, deciding to text Vera.

Ruby: I've made a huge mistake.
Vera: I think I know what you're talking about, but
just in case, you'd better tell me.

Ruby: Chase. I never should have pushed him away. And now I've been a big jerk. I'm sure it's too late.
Vera: You might be surprised, love.

49

Chase

On Sunday afternoon, Chase was sitting on his porch, staring off into the distance, when his phone rang. For a moment, he thought it might be Ruby. It was, however, her grandmother. He rolled his eyes at his momentary excitement. *It was obviously not going to be Ruby.*

"Hello?"

"Hello, Chase. How are you, dear? How was your show?"

"I'm okay. The show was amazing. The gallery owner called last night and said it was probably the most well-received show he's ever had. He said he would like to keep my work for an additional month *and* that there was a lot of purchasing interest."

"Wow. And to think, I have my own personal Chase Davidson painting. Nobody is getting their hands on it!" Ms. Millie laughed. For her most recent birthday, Chase had given her a small painting of a chipmunk on the forest floor. Chipmunks were her favorite animal.

Chase smiled for the first time since leaving the gallery. "If you have to start fending off would-be thieves, you let me know."

"I definitely will. But in the meantime, I was wondering if you could come over here? I need some help with my computer. I asked Gerald and he doesn't know how to help. Are you free now?"

"Sure, I can come over now. I'm going to let the dogs out for a few, then I'll head that way."

"Sounds good, sweetheart. Thanks so much."

• • • • •• • •• • • •

Chase made his way to the back side of the bakery. Ms. Millie met him outside and waved him into her RV.

"Thanks so much for coming so quickly. Technology is so helpful at times, but it also can be so frustrating."

Chase solved her problem in less than three minutes. "That's it, you're all set." *What now? I thought I would be here for a while.*

"I ordered a pizza a bit ago—it should be here anytime. You want to stay and have some?"

"Yeah, I'd love some. Thanks!" Chase was relieved to stay and enjoy the company of Ms. Millie. She gave him a familiar, homey feeling.

• • • • •• • • • •

After an hour or so of laughter and generally uplifting conversation, Chase headed home. He planned to work some and go to bed early. He found he felt better if he was either distracted or asleep. His brain was a messy place to be at the moment.

Chase pulled into his drive and got out of the car. He headed toward the door, but then he heard a sound. *Is that music? Where is that coming from?*

He headed toward the noise. When he rounded the corner to the backyard, his heart almost stopped. *Ruby.*

"Top of the mornin' to ya, Chase." Ruby walked toward him slowly, a small smile on her face. Chase stared, wide-eyed, as she came to a stop within arm's reach of him. "I was an idiot, Chase. I let my brain trick my heart into believing we couldn't or shouldn't be. I'm so sorry for the pain I'm sure I caused. And if it's too late, I understand. But I had to tell you that I love you. I don't know how or exactly when it happened, but it did. And I—"

Chase didn't let her finish. He enveloped her in his arms and crashed his lips to hers. He felt a tear escape, but he didn't care. *Ruby is here. She's really here.* He barely registered "Lovely Day" playing around them. He didn't have space for anything but her. He held her so tightly, he vaguely thought he should be concerned he would hurt her, but she wasn't complaining.

He picked her up and trailed kisses along her jaw before resting a damp cheek against hers and whispering into her ear. "I love you too, Ruby. I think I have, at least in a way, since the moment I saw you. You're like sunshine after years of clouds and rain. You've changed me and changed my life."

· · · · · ● · ● · · · ·

Once Chase came back to Earth, he noticed she had built a fire and had turned on the twinkle lights, even though there were at least a couple hours of sunlight left. Ruby grabbed his hand, pulling him toward the table. *I don't think I'll ever let go of this hand.*

"I made this for you," Ruby said, and Chase dragged his gaze from their linked hands to the table. There sat an apple pie. The top crust was cut to show their initials joined by a heart: R hearts C. "It's corny, but I had to do it."

"I love it so much. Maybe I'm into corny?" Chase smiled down at her, studying every aspect of her face. "I'm definitely into you."

Chase watched her cheeks take on a rosy hue, then kissed her again, but only briefly. "You said you didn't know when you fell in love with me, but for me it was when you came for breakfast. It was a simple night, but I had the best time. And I knew if you were mine, you would make even the simple times special." Ruby squeezed him and buried her face in his chest.

"You know," Chase continued, "maybe it was before then, when you did your horrible fake accent."

She backed from him and playfully hit him in the side. "It was extremely accurate and you know it."

"Whatever you say, Bee." Chase pulled her back to him, holding her close.

"I think for me, it was a slow build," Ruby said, rubbing circles on his back. "But maybe it was when you sent me flying into your dirty clothes basket."

"It could *not* have been that."

Ruby laughed. "No, but everything else that night. You were so sweet about everything." She sighed before she continued. "But now that I'm thinking about it, it may have been before that. I think I had to be really into you to agree to the prank, so maybe it was before then on the date. Things definitely changed for me then."

"So you're saying we may owe everything to the man smoking the pipe? Imagine if we had gone to his yacht party. We might already be married."

"Getting married, are we?" Ruby looked at him and raised an eyebrow.

Chase picked up the pie with one hand and took her hand again with the other, leading them toward his house. "You never do know, do ya Bee?"

As soon as they stepped inside the door, Ruby gasped. Chase watched her take in all the boxes he had packed since coming home from Vermont.

"Are you moving?"

"I think so. I decided on the way back from Vermont that I wasn't giving up on us. I planned to pack and show up at your door. If you wanted us, wanted me, I would've gotten a place near you. If you didn't, I was gonna go back to North Carolina."

Ruby launched herself into his arms. "Come to Vermont, Chase. I choose us. I want us. I want you."

50

Epilogue

A Year and a Half Later

Ruby

"Push, Ruby, push!"

Ruby groaned and pushed as best she could.

"Don't give up on me now!"

"What on earth makes you think I've given up?!" *He's about to tick me off. As if I'm not doing my best. Like we can just leave this big baby here.*

"That wasn't motivational?" Chase asked, leaning against his end of the armoire, peeking at Ruby through the door. The armoire was so large, it couldn't be lifted through the door—it could only be pushed and pulled.

"Maybe I don't respond well to that sort of motivation."

"Noted."

"We may need to call Gerald. I think I used all my strength helping get it to this point."

Ruby and Chase had gotten back from their honeymoon in Jamaica last week and were busy moving into their new home in Laurel Falls. They had lived in Vermont until their wedding, but Ruby had decided she missed Maine and Mamu and would love to go back to the place where she and Chase had fallen in love. When they'd looked into real estate in the area, they couldn't believe the house Chase had been living in previously was for sale. They snatched it up with a huge down payment. Chase's paintings had been doing extremely well. He had been feeling rather inspired. He had even been able to stop his work as a massage therapist. Apart from massages for Ruby, who required at least two a week.

Ruby heard a noise and turned to see Mamu and Gerald heading down the drive. "Thank goodness," she whispered to herself. They got out of the car, Gerald carrying a couple pizzas and Mamu a six-pack of sparkling black cherry water.

"Moving day sustenance!" Mamu called as they approached.

"To get inside, you guys have to push this armoire through the door," Ruby said, as if it were the only option.

"We *could* go in through the screened porch," Mamu responded with feigned attitude.

"Only if you want to break my heart and possibly my back."

"You guys are so sweet together. I'm going to push the armoire," Gerald interjected. "Ready, Chase?"

"Yep!" Chase's voice called from inside.

Before long, Chase and Gerald had the huge piece of furniture inside and in place. They relaxed on the screened porch, enjoying their moving day sustenance.

"I'm so glad you guys are back here. I've missed you both so much," Mamu said, leaning back in her chair. "When I initiated my plan to get you guys married, I hoped you would be here, but I thought it was a long shot."

"So you finally admit it!" Ruby exclaimed, pointing an accusatory finger at her grandmother. "You're a schemer!" Mamu simply raised her shoulders in a shrug.

"Wow. Seems like you're pretty upset about it. I'm hurt," Chase said with raised eyebrows.

Ruby turned to Chase and softened. She moved to him and sat in his lap. "I've never been less upset about anything in my entire life." She kissed his cheek and settled in to stay.

Chase turned to whisper in her ear, "And *I've* never been happier in my entire life. You're my favorite, Bee."

"And you're mine."

Upcoming

Do you love Vera? Want more?

Wonder who she might fall for in Autumn 2023?

It just might be Luca Bello, the newest resident of Mamu's

apartment. Keep a look out for her book this fall!

Autumn in Laurel Falls

Winter in Laurel Falls

Spring in Laurel Falls

Please leave a review on Amazon and/or Goodreads. It's the most

important thing you can do for an indie author.

Thanks in advance!!!

Interested in some recipes from the book?

Head to LindsayRochester.com and sign up for my newsletter!

Acknowledgements

I kept the fact that I was writing a novel a secret because if I failed, I didn't want it to be a big deal. Because of that, my dad never knew I was writing this. He died unexpectedly during the early stages of writing. I'll tell him one day, though.

Thank you, Dad. Thank you for being you and being a part of helping me become who I am today. I like to think some of your humor made its way into this book. I miss you.

Thank you to my family (husband, children, mother, mother-in-love, father-in-love, and special friends), for your support, belief and honesty. I'm pretty sure you're not lying to me when you say this book is really good!

Thank you to my earliest readers. Especially those who told me, "Honestly, I'm surprised at how good it is." This cracks me up because I surprised myself as well.

Tay, my first reader, my reading buddy, thank you. You gave me the confidence to keep going.

Susan, when you told me you loved it, my jaw hit the floor. I had fully expected you to "let me down gently." Your words of wisdom and guidance meant the world to me. Thank you.

Mary Frances, you literary genius, thank you so much for your feedback. It was exactly what I needed. And I can't tell you how much I appreciate you writing the blurb. I just couldn't do it!

Karen, it thrills me that you are already excited for the next book! Thank you for reading and making me feel more solid in my decision to publish.

Sydney, thank you for stepping outside your normal genre and reading. You gave some of the most specific feedback and I loved it!

Fran, you called me an author and I still can't believe it's true. As with everything, you were so helpful and good. (And thank you for finding all the places I made Ruby sound southern, OOPS.)

Mom, thank you for helping us make this happen. It's made this process a lot less stressful! Thank you for being you and helping me become me.

D, you're my very favorite, even if you stopped reading my first draft because you couldn't deal with my grammatical errors. You'll read it once I put a paperback in your hands, right? :) I appreciate your support and belief more than you know. This is pretty exciting, huh?!